Stepping Stones

4 vmbo-gt

Activity Book B

Daniëlle Derkse

Arne van Diemen

Eppe Scholtens

Mirjam Versteeg

Eindredactie: Elien Cusveller

Native speaker eindredactie: Jennifer Purcell

Vijfde editie

Noordhoff Uitgevers

Stepping Stones 4 vmbo-gt bestaat uit:

- *Textbook* = bronnenboek
- *Activity Books 4A* en *4B*
- *Stepping Stones online*, met
  - voor de leerling: onder andere al het audio- en videomateriaal
  - extra voor de docent: onder andere toetsen, tapescripts, uitwerkingen en een presentatietool voor het digitale schoolbord

Wij besteden veel zorg aan de ontwikkeling van onze leermiddelen en doen er alles aan om fouten te voorkomen. Mocht u onverhoopt toch een fout tegenkomen, dan kunt u dit per mail doorgeven aan steppingstones@noordhoff.nl.

Met dank aan Anja Borman, Adriënne Buschmann, Edith van 't Wout

Vormgeving omslag Conceptontwerp: Fabrique, Communicatie en design, Delft / Vertaling ontwerp De Weijer Design BNO, Baarn
Omslagillustratie De Weijer Design BNO, Baarn
Omslagfoto Imagedock
Vormgeving binnenwerk Bloemvis, Groningen
Illustraties Geza Illustraties, Heiloo

Bronvermelding
Getty Images: p. 6, 51 l
Shutterstock: p. 28, 51 r
Corbis: p. 62, 87, 107
iStockphoto: p. 79
Imageselect, Wassenaar: p. 98

MIX
Papier van verantwoorde herkomst
FSC® C118189
FSC www.fsc.org

4 / 19

ISBN 978-90-01-83694-8

Table of contents

ERK

ERK leerdoelen

Uitleg van de symbolen

Bij deze opdracht ga je luisteren.

Bij deze opdracht ga je een videoclip bekijken.

Ga naar *Stepping Stones online* voor meer opdrachten.

Deze opdracht doe je met zijn tweeën.

Deze opdracht doe je in een groepje.

Deze opdracht is voor je taalportfolio.

Instructions used

Boven elke opdracht staat in een Engelse zin wat je moet doen. Als je niet begrijpt wat je bij een opdracht moet doen, kijk je in deze lijst. Na een tijdje ken je waarschijnlijk al deze zinnen.

Answer the questions	*Beantwoord de vragen*
Choose the correct alternative	*Kies de juiste mogelijkheid*
Choose the correct answer	*Kies het juiste antwoord*
Choose the odd one out	*Kies het woord dat er niet bij past*
Complete the article	*Maak het artikel af*
Complete the conversation	*Maak het gesprek af*
Complete the dialogue	*Maak het gesprek af*
Complete the email	*Maak de e-mail af*
Complete the forum	*Maak het forum af*
Complete the sentences	*Maak de zinnen af*
Complete the *Stone*	*Maak de Stone af*
Complete the text	*Maak de tekst af*
Correct the mistakes	*Verbeter de fouten*
Create a puzzle	*Maak een puzzel*
Do the quiz	*Doe de quiz*
Fill in	*Vul in*
Fill in the fact file	*Vul de fact file in*
Fill in the grid	*Vul het schema in*
Fill in the mind map	*Vul de woordspin in*
Fill in the words	*Vul de woorden in*
Guess the words	*Raad de woorden*
Make the correct combinations	*Maak de juiste combinaties*
Play the role	*Speel de rol*
Put in the correct order	*Zet in de juiste volgorde*
Say it in English	*Zeg het in het Engels*
Solve the puzzle	*Los de puzzel op*
Talk to a classmate	*Praat met een klasgenoot*
Tick the boxes	*Kruis de hokjes aan*
True or false?	*Waar of niet waar?*
Write (down) the questions	*Schrijf de vragen (op)*
Write (down) the sentences	*Schrijf de zinnen (op)*
Write (down) the words	*Schrijf de woorden (op)*
Write a description	*Schrijf een omschrijving*
Write a letter	*Schrijf een brief*
Write an email	*Schrijf een e-mail*
Write down	*Schrijf op*

Grammatical terms

Belangrijke woordsoorten

(hoofd)werkwoord (ww) = verb	George **is** 13 years old.
hulpwerkwoord (hww) = auxiliary verb	I **can** help. Of course you **may** use my phone. We **could** play a game. You **should** do your homework. We **have to** write a book report.
infinitief/hele werkwoord = infinitive	Do you need a hand? I'm happy to **help**.
zelfstandig naamwoord (zn) = noun	Our **car** is blue.
bijvoeglijk naamwoord (bn) = adjective	We have got a **big** house.
bijwoord (bw) = adverb	My trainers are **bright** blue.
lidwoord (lw) = article	My brother has got **a** leather jacket.

Zinsontleding

onderwerp (ow) = subject	**We** could give him a new video game. *(wie/wat + gezegde?)*
persoonsvorm (pv) = finite verb	She **walks** home every day. *(enkelvoud, tegenwoordige tijd)* She **walked** home every day. *(enkelvoud, verleden tijd)*
gezegde = predicate	We **could give** him a new video game.
lijdend voorwerp (lv) = direct object	We could give him **a new video game**. *(wie/wat + gezegde + onderwerp?)*
meewerkend voorwerp (mv) = indirect object	We could give **him** a new video game. *(aan/voor wie + gezegde + onderwerp + lijdend voorwerp?)*

When you have finished the exercises in this theme...

you can

- talk about finding out how things work
- make predictions
- A2 I can write about everyday aspects of my life in sentences that are properly connected.
- A2 I can give a short, prepared presentation about a topic in my everyday life.
- B1 I can write a short, simple report in a set format.

you understand

- words to do with the mind and science
- words to do with tricks and experiments

you know

- how to use all the verb tenses you have learned so far
- how to use *if-sentences*

Test Yourself

Do the *Test Yourself* at the end of the theme (in your *Activity Book* or in *Stepping Stones online*) and check whether you're ready for the test.

ERK

Reading/listening: B1 B2 / A1 B2
Speaking/writing: A2 / A2 B1

4 Can you believe it?

1 Make the correct combinations

In the next exercise the topic is learning styles. There are three types of learners. Match the statements with the correct type of learner. One statement will be left over. Draw lines.

Listening learner	learns by just looking at how things should be done.
Seeing learner	tries to discover how to do things just by doing it.
Experience learner	reads and writes about what he / she has learnt.
	wants to hear what he / she has to do.

Now do the quiz *What kind of learner are you?* on page 82 in your Textbook.

What type of learner are you? I am a(n) ______________________________ learner.

2 Choose the correct alternative

Listen to *Learning styles.* Choose the correct answers. There are pauses.

Strategy In this exercise you will practise *listening intently* (intensief luisteren). Listen to the fragment and try to understand all the information.

1 What does Jamie want to make clear to Mr Gibson?
- A ❑ That he will have better results when he is allowed to listen to music.
- B ❑ That his school results are better than Mr Gibson thinks.
- C ❑ That some types of music are more helpful in studying than others.

2 What does Rick make clear about his uncle?
- A ❑ He has become so rich that he doesn't need to read anything anymore.
- B ❑ He has learned what he needed to know by doing things.
- C ❑ It took him much longer than others to become a good reader.

3 What does Mr Gibson say about himself?
- A ❑ That he wanted to be something else than a language teacher.
- B ❑ That he was different than what Maria expected.
- C ❑ Why he was always misbehaving.

4 What does Mr Gibson want to make clear about the documentary he saw?
- A ❑ How different types of learners tackle problems.
- B ❑ That lots of people do not listen carefully enough.
- C ❑ That people often make mistakes by learning the wrong way.

5 How does Rick react to what Mr Gibson says about types of learners?
- A ❑ He disagrees with Mr Gibson's theories completely.
- B ❑ He says that pupils should have more freedom on how to learn.
- C ❑ He thinks there are teachers who have no idea what learning really is.

6 What is Mr Gibson's reaction?
- A ❑ He disagrees with both Rick and Maria.
- B ❑ He does exactly what Rick wants him to do.
- C ❑ He is not satisfied with the pupils' results for English.

3 Make the correct combinations

Look at *Theme words* on page 82 of your *Textbook*. Match the *Theme words* with the correct descriptions. Write the letters in the correct order in the box below.

1	The way you act or respond to something.	C	intuition
2	Feelings of disorientation.	L	imagination
3	A natural feeling you have inside.	A	optical illusion
4	You use these to see, hear, taste or feel things.	T	behaviour
5	Science that focuses on the mind and behavior.	C	disguise
6	A camouflage that hides something.	O	confusion
7	Something that takes your attention away.	O	senses
8	When your sight tricks you.	N	psychology
9	The ability to form a picture in your mind.	E	distraction

1	2	3	4	5	6	7	8	9

The word in the grid is: ....

In Dutch this means: ....

4 Fill in the words

Fill in the missing *Theme words.* Choose from the words below.

flabbergasted – to grasp – magician – to manipulate – to react – trickery

Back Forward Stop Refresh Home Search Favorites History Mail Print

Agenda | Restaurants | Drinks | Magazines | **Forum**

Topic: Books about magic tricks

Mr_Magic

Posted at 11:35am on June 23

Hi there!

I was wondering if somebody can help me out. I'm looking for a book which can tell me more about becoming a **(1)** .... I have always been interested in **(2)** .... and fooling people. I especially like it when people are not able **(3)** ....my tricks and walk away

(4) ________________________________ It makes me laugh a little, because I know that it's all fake. In my opinion the best thing about doing tricks is that I can create the illusion that I have the power **(5)** ________________________________ objects. If you are into doing tricks as well, feel free **(6)** ________________________________ to this message. Maybe we can teach each other some new things!

Bye,

Christopher

C

READING

5 Write down

Read the first paragraph of *Rising star: Troy Von Scheibner* on page 83 of your *Textbook*. Then scan the text and write down what the terms and names below refer to.

! **Strategy** In this exercise you will practise *scanning* a text (zoekend lezen). Look for specific information in the text. Read the title, and look for distinct words such as numbers and words with capital letters.

1 12 ______
2 15 ______
3 26 ______
4 David Blaine ______
5 Magic Boy ______
6 Parlour Skate Store ______
7 South London ______
8 top hats and a cape ______

6 True or false?

Read *Rising star: Troy Von Scheibner* again. Indicate whether the statements are true or false.

		true	false
1	Troy uses jewels and other fashion items in his tricks.	❏	❏
2	Troy's father helped Troy to get started in the world of magic.	❏	❏
3	At university Troy noticed that people expect you to be a magician all the time.	❏	❏
4	Troy makes a pack of cards disappear when shuffling them.	❏	❏
5	The author of the article is annoyed that Troy refuses to explain the card trick.	❏	❏
6	According to Troy it is very important for magicians to interact well with people when they are performing.	❏	❏

7 Solve the puzzle

Have a look at *Rising star: Troy Von Scheibner* again. Translate the Dutch words and put the translations in the puzzle. You can find the words in the text.

1 schudden ______
2 stapel ______
3 ongemakkelijk ______
4 ondeugend ______
5 ouderwets ______
6 dwarszitten ______
7 toch ______
8 verwerken ______

Which word can you read in the grey boxes? ______

In Dutch this means: ______

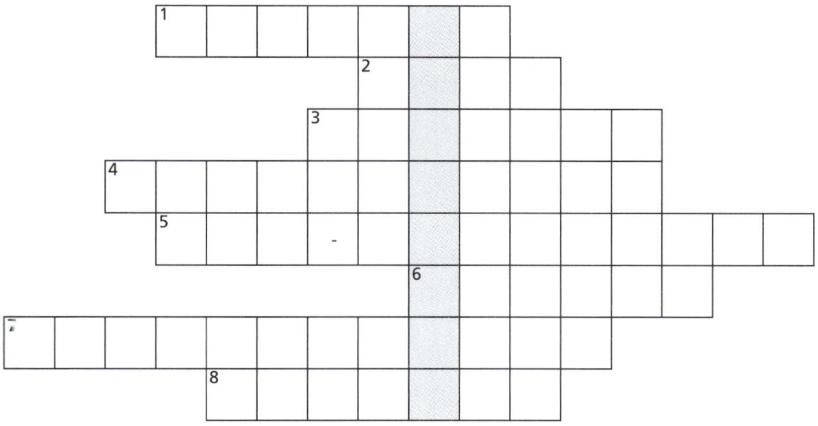

8 Write the sentences

Study *Stone 10* on page 84 of your *Textbook*. Have a look at the pictures.
Write a sentence below each picture using the words between brackets.

(mijn doel – uitzoeken – of mensen – zouden stelen – of teruggeven – nieuwste smartphone)

....

....

....

(instrueerde – klasgenoot – hoe – laten vallen)

....

....

....

(lette goed op – hoe – mensen – reageerden – en schreef op)

....

....

....

(klasgenoot – beweert – meeste mensen – eerlijk)

....

....

....

D
SPEAKING
WRITING

9 Complete the text

Complete the text. Use the clues between brackets and the *Stone*.

All about the mind

This is our report about a little 'mind experiment' we did for our school project. Our teacher instructed us to do an experiment about something we found interesting ourselves.

(1) ______________________________

______________________ (*we waren benieuwd – hoe – mensen – beste leren*)

We believe we're not the best students, so maybe we could learn something by the learning styles of our classmates and teachers.

(2) ______________________________

______________________ (*hoe bepalen – welke manier – ze – studeren?*)

At first we didn't know how we should find this out. We discussed it with our teacher and soon we had it figured out.

We **(3)** ______________________________

______________________ (*vroegen – twintig klasgenoten en tien leraren – enquête invullen – waar en hoe ze studeren*)

We also asked them about their favourite learning styles. **(4)** ______________________

______________________ (*alle deelnemers moesten – hun favoriete leerstijlen – juiste volgorde zetten*)

Results

The results were quite interesting. **(5)** ______________________

______________________ (*veel klasgenoten – zeiden – beste concentreren – hun slaapkamer*)

(6) ______________________________

______________________ (*anderen beweerden – beste leerden – als – praten*) about it.

The results were different for the teachers.

(7) ______________________________

______________________ (*meeste leraren zeiden – beste concentreren – door – lezen*)

So it seems that the learning styles of young people (our classmates) are different from those of older people (the teachers). Isn't that interesting?

D
SPEAKING
WRITING

E
GRAMMAR

10 Play the role

Work with a classmate. Decide who is pupil A and who is pupil B.

Pupil A   Speech card 17   Pupil B   Speech card 22

Look up your speech card in *Talking Matters* at the back of your *Activity Book*.

11 Choose the correct alternative

Study *Grammar 10* on page 85 of your *Textbook*. Circle the correct answer.

1 How on earth did he do that trick? I *will ask / am asking* him when I see him again.
2 Andy *prepares / is preparing* for his magic act at the moment. You shouldn't disturb him.
3 *Do they attend / Are they going to attend* the psychology conference in July?
4 Courtney *does / is doing* yoga exercises every morning.
5 The mind-reading documentary *starts / is going to start* in ten minutes. I really want to see it!
6 I expect these brain training games *will help / are helping* you concentrate.
7 After he *solved / had solved* the puzzle, John felt really proud of himself.
8 Stage magicians *have always fascinated / always fascinated* Everett since he was a kid.
9 Why *weren't you paying attention / haven't you paid attention* when the magician showed his tricks?
10 Sean *was practising / has practised* with his brain training app when another pupil interrupted him.
11 I *looked / have looked* at this optical illusion for quite a while now, but I still don't know how it works.
12 *Did you notice / had you noticed* the distraction techniques he used during last night's show?

12 Complete the forum

Complete the forum by filling in the correct tense. Use the words between brackets. Sometimes more answers are correct. Use *Grammar 10*.

Back Forward Stop Refresh Home Search Favorites History Mail Print

Agenda | Restaurants | Drinks | Magazines | **Forum**

Topic: Tricks to fool my friends

LawrenceLarge: Everybody **(1)** ______________________ (*know*) that magicians also use psychological tricks to fool people and not just their quick hands. Well, right now I **(2)** ______________________ (*look*) for mind-games tricks to try on my friends. Have you got any suggestions?

E GRAMMAR

Sunflower99:	Make someone feel insecure by looking at their hairline while they speak. I did this one last week and it **(3)** ______________ (*work*) like a charm. I'm sure you **(4)** ______________ (*have*) much fun with this one ;-)
KendallJ:	What about this? If somebody **(5)** ______________ (*try*) to count something, you should say numbers in an order (for example 2, 4, 6 8) because the brain thinks in patterns. I **(6)** ______________ (*do*) this a couple of times. It will totally confuse them!
Carol_coral:	If you want to get rid of an object and want someone else to carry it, just keep talking to that person while handing him the object. Most of the times people will just take the object automatically without thinking. I **(7)** ______________ (*try*) this trick yesterday when my friend and I **(8)** ______________ (*walk*) home from the supermarket store. I gave him this heavy gallon of milk while talking to him and he accepted it without any protest! After I **(9)** ______________ (*tell*) my friend about this trick, he just **(10)** ______________ *(laugh)* about it... luckily ;-)

Adapted from lifebuzz.com

F WATCHING

13 Choose the correct alternative

Read the statements carefully. Then watch *Selling it right*. Choose the correct alternative.

1 A ❑ A 'blue chip' company refers to a very famous international business.
  B ❑ A 'blue chip' company refers to any business that wants to do a digital campaign.

2 A ❑ One of Simon's responsibilities is to find and approach new clients.
  B ❑ Simon has to decide what steps should be taken in a specific project.

3 A ❑ The campaign for the sneakers focussed on characters in ads wearing the shoes.
  B ❑ The campaign for the sneakers focussed on showing the shoe as much as possible.

4 A ❑ In campaigns you have to be popular on social media channels to be successful.
  B ❑ In campaigns you have to come up with interesting stories to make a product appealing.

5 A ❑ Successful campaigns are the ones that have a positive message.
  B ❑ Successful campaigns understand the target group's world and lifestyle.

6 A ❑ Agencies in Amsterdam are popular because it is one of the most creative cities in the world.
B ❑ Agencies in Amsterdam are popular because they know what works in international campaigns.

G
LISTENING

14 Answer the questions

Read *Mind-blowing tricks* on page 86 in your Textbook. Answer the questions in Dutch.

1 Naar welke vaardigheid verwijst de term '*mindreading*'?

2 Wat kun je leren in de workshop?

3 Voor wie is de workshop precies bedoeld?

15 Put in the correct order

Read the sentences below carefully. Then listen to *Mind-blowing tricks.* Put the sentences in the order of the text by writing the numbers 1 to 6 in front of the sentences. There are no pauses.

Strategy In this exercise you will practise recognising intonation (*intonatie*). Pay special attention to the speakers' tone. This may help you find out how the speakers are feeling or what they mean.

❑ Michael legt uit hoe de trucs werken.
❑ Jennifer zoekt de juiste naam op in het telefoonboek.
❑ Jennifer is erg verbaasd dat Michael de juiste soort groente noemde.
❑ Jennifer vraagt zich af of Michael werkelijk gedachten kan lezen.
❑ Michael vertelt dat '*mindreading*' niet veel meer is dan een truc.
❑ Jennifer vertelt waarom haar workshop erg interessant was.

H
READING

16 Answer the questions

Read the first paragraph of *Grocery shopping and ordering whoppers* on page 86 of your *Textbook*. Answer the questions in Dutch.

1 Welke situatie wordt in de eerste alinea beschreven?

2 Welke sociale norm wordt hier doorbroken (alinea 2)?

3 Wat is het doel van '*breaching experiments*' (alinea 2)?

4 Lees nu de rest van de tekst. Schrijf nog vier andere voorbeelden van *'breaching experiments'* op die worden genoemd.

5 Probeer nog twee voorbeelden van *'breaching experiments'* te bedenken die niet in de tekst voorkomen, maar die je ergens hebt gezien of misschien zelf hebt meegemaakt.

17 Make the correct combinations

Read *Grocery shopping and ordering whoppers* again. Draw lines to match the words on the left to the information from the text.

Garfinkel	asked for explanation about behaviour
breaching experiment	Burger King
students' parents	looking for help from colleagues
students	difficult task at home
Whopper	invented breaching experiment
clerk	programme with breaching experiments
Punk'd	simple to do and cheap

18 Choose the correct alternative

Read *Grocery shopping and ordering whoppers* again. Answer the questions.

Strategy In this exercise you will practise filling in gaps in the text. Read the sentences before and after the gap and try to think of a word that could fit the blank space. Then read the options and choose the best one.

1 Which of the following words fits the gap at __1__?
A ❑ friendly environment
B ❑ serious emergency
C ❑ unusual situation

2 Which of the following words fits the gap at __2__?
A ❑ broken
B ❑ respected
C ❑ shared

3 Which of the following words fits the gap at __3__?
A ❑ Above all
B ❑ However
C ❑ In the first place

H READING

I SPEAKING WRITING

4 Which of the following words fits the gap at __4__?
A ❑ embarrassed and ashamed at
B ❑ anxious and worried by
C ❑ upset and confused at

5 Which of the following words fits the gap at __5__?
A ❑ expensive
B ❑ important
C ❑ ridiculous

6 Which of the following words fits the gap at __6__?
A ❑ For example
B ❑ Furthermore
C ❑ However

19 Make the correct combinations

Study *Stone 11* on page 88 of your *Textbook*. Make correct sentences by using one phrase from each column. Then write down the Dutch translations.

I'm convinced they will	will live well into their hundreds	better at tests.
It's likely that	create computers	by 2150.
If you use brain training games you	twenty years' time meditation exercises	reveal everything you know.
Studies suggest that in	might perform	will be in everyone's daily routine.
In 50 years' time no	one will use	with human intelligence.
We're certain most people	brain scans will be able to	computers anymore.

1 EN ______________________________

NL ______________________________

2 EN ______________________________

NL ______________________________

3 EN ______________________________

NL ______________________________

4 EN ______________________________

NL ______________________________

5 EN ______________________________

NL ______________________________

6 EN ______________________________

NL ______________________________

20 Complete the dialogue

Look at *Stone 11* again. Complete the dialogue. Use the clues in brackets.

Maureen: Hey Matt, what are you doing? Are you installing a new app?

Matt: Yes, this is a new brain training game. They say that **(1)** ______________________________ (*als – je – het gebruikt – zult hebben – betere studieresultaten*).

Maureen: Does it really work?

Matt: **(2)** ______________________________ (*onderzoek wijst uit – maakt schoolwerk – gemakkelijker*).
Some people even think these games are more important than teachers. They can really help you with memorising things and stuff like that.

Maureen: You mean that **(3)** ______________________________
(*deze spellen die je hersenen trainen – leraren zullen vervangen – spoedig?*)
That would be cool... No more boring lessons but just games to get better at learning.

Matt: I'm not sure if that will happen, but **(4)** ______________________________ (*voorspel – ze – dit jaar – populairder worden*). As a matter of fact, **(5)** ______________________________
(*verwacht – iedereen – ze zal gebruiken – vijf jaar tijd*).

Maureen: Do you really think so? Well, I guess there are stranger things that can happen.

Matt: What do you mean by that?

Maureen: I read this magazine the other day and they had made a list of predictions about the future. It was really weird. The authors of the magazine think that
(6) ______________________________ (*in vijftien jaar – computers – in staat zullen zijn zich te gedragen – net als mensen*).
Also, they think **(7)** ______________________________
(*erg aannemelijk – mensen – in de ruimte zullen wonen – volgende eeuw*)
What surprised me most was that **(8)** ______________________________ (*zeker – robots – mensen zullen vervangen – verre toekomst*)

Matt: What do you mean?

Maureen: They think that they will take over our jobs because they can do tasks much more efficiently than us.

Matt: That means no more jobs and more spare time for us. That's just perfect, robots taking over... I'm all for it!

Now act out the conversation with a classmate.

21 Write the post

Read the text below. Next, write a response.
Make sure you:
- write down at least four predictions about the future. You can make these up yourself
- write 60 to 80 words
- use *Stone 11*

Back Forward Stop Refresh Home Search Favorites History Mail Print

Agenda | Restaurants | Drinks | Magazines | **Forum**

Topic: the future of things to come

Peter2000

How far will technology advance in 20, 30, even 50 years from now? How will it change our lives? What do you think? I've created this blog because I'm curious how other people think about the future. Please send me your predictions!
Peter.

J GRAMMAR

22 Make the correct combinations

Study *Grammar 11* on page 89 of your *Textbook*. Make correct sentences by drawing lines.

If scientists made robots with emotions	you will go crazy.
I will leave the theatre	you would fail.
If you look at a red dot a long time,	you will see it everywhere.
If you stay awake for too long,	if I miss the nine o'clock bus.
If you looked at his hand movements	if the magician keeps messing up his tricks.
If you took a lie detector test,	it would be a great scientific breakthrough.
If you run a marathon	you would notice how the trick worked.
I will be late for my brain scan	you should mentally prepare for it.

23 Write the sentences

Write correct if-sentences using the clues and the pictures. Use *Grammar 11*. Sometimes there is more than one way to make correct sentences.

fact: schrijf een if-zin voor feiten
will: schrijf een if-zin met will
would: schrijf een zin if-zin met would

1

Example

will (*stop – raining – walk*)

If it stops raining I will go outside for a walk.

2

fact (*freeze – water – turn to*)

3

would (*John – promoted – a big party*)

4

fact (*you – mix – get – green*)

5

would (*Sam – lottery – cruise*)

6

will (*her boyfriend – not call back – soon – mad*)

J GRAMMAR

K WATCHING

24 Complete the sentences

Read *Moving legs* on page 89 in your *Textbook*. Finish the sentences.

1 According to the text, insects are not ______, but ______

2 Researchers in Chile are doing experiments using the ______ of a ______

3 The researchers are trying to ______

25 Choose the best alternative

Watch *Moving legs.* Indicate which translation of the words is in line with the text in the clip. There are pauses after each two words.

! **Strategy** In this exercise you will practise tackling difficult words (*moeilijke woorden*). While listening, you sometimes come across difficult words which you need to understand the fragment. You can often guess their meaning, for instance because you recognise part of the word, or by listening carefully to the context.

1 *to interface with*
A ❑ koppelen aan
B ❑ veranderen met

2 *to control*
A ❑ besturen
B ❑ in de gaten houden

3 *capture*
A ❑ begrijpen
B ❑ vastleggen

4 *fashion*
A ❑ manier
B ❑ mode

5 *impulses*
A ❑ stofjes
B ❑ prikkels

6 *detects*
A ❑ onderzoeken
B ❑ waarnemen

7 *converting*
A ❑ omzetten
B ❑ uitschakelen

8 *implications*
A ❑ gevolgen
B ❑ problemen

Test Yourself ✔

Study the *Vocabulary*, *Grammar*, and *Stones*.
Then do the *Test Yourself* below.

You can also do the *Test Yourself* in *Stepping Stones online*. If necessary, it will refer you to extra online exercises to prepare you for the test.

1 Vocabulary

Fill in the correct word.

Choose from: beforehand – charm – coincidence – furious – identify – ignorant – manipulate – trickery

Professional con-artist swindles **(1)** ______________ people.
Three men, who sold fake lottery tickets on the streets, were arrested by the police yesterday. Witnesses said that the men looked reliable because they had a company card with them and wore suits. They also said that one of the men had a natural **(2)** ______________ and was very friendly.

The police explained that con-artists often choose their victims **(3)** ______________ and try to **(4)** ______________ them.
Unfortunately this kind of **(5)** ______________ is happening more and more.
A police spokesman stated that it is not a **(6)** ______________ that as many as three suspects were arrested because they often work in a bigger network.

The money, which the con-artists took from the victims, is still nowhere to be found.
Some of the victims are **(7)** ______________ because they have lost their money. One man said he bought lottery tickets with a total amount of £300.

Victims who have been swindled are asked to contact the police on 5953 and **(8)** ______________ the con-artists.

2 Grammar

Choose the correct form of the verb.

1 I ________________ (*always – dream*) of going to the *Comic Con* with my best friend.

2 My friends and I ________________ (*not – go*) to the magic festival in Cardiff last month.

3 Yesterday the teacher ________________ (*explain*) the exercise when Ron ________________ (*start*) laughing.

4 Our train ________________ (*depart*) in fifteen minutes from platform 6.

5 Before he ________________ (*become*) an artist he ________________ (*be*) a manager.

6 She ________________ (*pass*) her scooter exam. That's why she ________________ (*drive*) her scooter right now.

7 Diana ________________ (*not – come*) to the party because she ________________ (*be*) ill for three days.

8 We ________________ (*host*) a live performance of my favourite magician this Saturday.

9 He ________________ (*say*) he ________________ (*not – do*) the *Mindreading* workshop before.

10 We ________________ (*work*) on our presentation before we (*go*) ________________ to the cinema last night.

3 Grammar

Fill in the correct form of the verb in brackets.

1 If I ________________ (*find*) a wallet, I would take it to the police.

2 The scientists will find a cure, if they ________________ (*receive*) more money.

3 You ________________ (*arrive*) early if you leave now.

4 If you press this button, the alarm ________________ (*go*) off.

5 If Shahira ________________ (*walk*) to the workshop right now, she will be on time.

6 Troy wouldn't perform if he ________________ (*be*) ill.

7 If you train your brain regularly you ________________ (*feel*) better.

8 People wouldn't gain more weight if they ________________ (*exercise*) on a daily basis.

9 Water ________________ (*boil*) if you heat it to 100 degrees Celsius.

10 If I ________________ (*have*) a lot of money, I would buy a sports car.

4 Stones

Say it in English.

1 Ik wilde uitzoeken hoe zijn truc met de tijgers werkt.

2 Sarah beweert dat ze zich alleen kan concentreren wanneer ze kauwgom kauwt.

3 Wij gaan een aantal klasgenoten ondervragen over de manier waarop ze studeren.

4 In de verre toekomst zullen mensen in staat zijn op de maan te wonen.

5 Ik ben ervan overtuigd dat er tegen 2050 een geneesmiddel voor veel ziekten zal zijn.

6 Wij verwachten dat spellen die je hersens trainen minder populair zullen worden.

7 Ze zegt dat ze zich niet beter kan concentreren wanneer ze naar muziek luistert.

8 Ik vroeg een aantal mensen hun feedback op te schrijven.

	OK!	Herhaling (bladzijde 52-54)
Vocabulary	❑ 0-3 ft	❑ meer dan 3 ft → opdracht 1, 2
Grammar	❑ 0-6 ft	❑ meer dan 6 ft → opdracht 3, 4
Stones	❑ 0-3 ft	❑ meer dan 3 ft → opdracht 5, 6

Let hierbij ook goed op je spelling!

Heb je overal OK aangekruist? Ga dan naar *Verrijking* op bladzijde 55.

Task

>> TASKCARD

Senses survey
Je gaat een onderzoek doen naar hoe je zintuigen beïnvloed kunnen worden.

(A2) Ik kan schrijven over alledaagse aspecten van mijn omgeving in zinnen die met elkaar verbonden zijn.
(A2) Ik kan een korte, ingestudeerde presentatie geven over een onderwerp uit mijn dagelijks leven.
(B1) Ik kan een kort, eenvoudig verslag schrijven volgens een vast format.

ERK

STEP 1

Preparation

Look at the *Task* on page 90 of your *Textbook*. In this *Task* you are going to research how your senses can be influenced.

- Study *Stones 10* and *11* on pages 84 and 88 of your *Textbook*.
- Learn the words from the *Vocabulary* on pages 91 to 93 of your *Textbook*.

! **Tip** First read the sentences under *Step 4: Evaluation* on page 27. Keep these points in mind when doing your *Task*.

STEP 2

Orientation

Read *The smell report* on page 90 of your *Textbook*.

1 Tick the boxes of the items that are mentioned in the report.

- ❑ a description of the research question
- ❑ when the research took place
- ❑ how they set up the research
- ❑ why people participated in it
- ❑ the number of participants
- ❑ what sort of question participants had to answer
- ❑ the outcome of the research

2 This *Task* is called *Sense survey*. How many senses (*zintuigen*) do we have? Write them down in Dutch. Then translate them into English.

NL ______________________________

EN ______________________________

STEP 3

Realisation

1 Work together with a classmate. You're going to set up your own research project about how senses (*zintuigen*) influence your behaviour.

We want to find out how ______________________________

influences ______________________________

! **Tip** Read the Theme again to get inspired!

2 Together fill in the details of your research project in English.
Make sure you:
- can carry out your research in a short time.
- get a total of 10 results that you can write about in your report (for example by handing out questionnaires to people or by doing interviews).

What do we want to test?	
How are we going to test it?	
What do we think will be the outcome of the test?	

3 Make sure you have all the material you need (for example a list of songs, a number of questionnaires) and carry out your research.

4 Collect all the results and write a short report like *The smell report* in your *Textbook*. Use at least 120 words for writing your research report. You can write it on a separate piece of paper or on the computer.

5 Did you expect this outcome? Explain your answer.

....

....

6 Work together with another couple. Give a short presentation about your research. Your classmates will ask you questions about your research. Answer their questions. After that, the other couple will present their research to you.

STEP 4

Evaluation

Work together with your classmate and discuss how you've done. Indicate whether each sentence is true or false.

	true	false
We used words from the *Vocabulary*.	❑	❑
We used words and sentences from the *Stones*.	❑	❑
We filled in the details of our research.	❑	❑
We asked 10 different people several questions.	❑	❑
We wrote a research report.	❑	❑
We presented our research to another couple.	❑	❑
We answered the questions of another couple.	❑	❑
We asked another couple questions.	❑	❑

Keep (a copy of) your research report in your language portfolio.

When you have finished the exercises in this theme...

you can
- make comparisons
- ask for and give clarifications
- talk about facts and convictions
- A2 B1 I can make comparisons in a simple and describing manner and make short statements about things and possessions.
- A2 B1 I can describe everyday aspects in my surroundings.

you understand
- words to do with the language and convictions
- words to do with comparisons

you know
- how to use *comparatives* and *superlatives* (trappen van vergelijking)
- how to use *complex* and *compound sentences* (samengestelde en complexe zinnen)
- how to use *relative clauses* (betrekkelijke bijzinnen)

Test Yourself

Do the *Test Yourself* at the end of the theme (in your *Activity Book* or in *Stepping Stones online*) and check whether you're ready for the test.

ERK

Reading/listening: B1 B2 / A2 B1
Speaking/writing: A2 / A2 B1

5 English around the world

A
LISTENING

1 Choose the correct answer

Read *An English quiz* on page 96 in your *Textbook*. Answer the quiz questions. Write down the correct letter. You can find the correct answers at the bottom of this page.

1 .... 2 .... 3 .... 4 ....

2 Choose the correct alternative

Listen to *Quiz Time*. Choose the correct answer to the questions. There are pauses.

Strategy In this exercise you will practise *listening intently* (intensief luisteren). Listen to the fragment and try to understand all the information.

1 A ❑ Sabrina, Josie and Amir think differently about the answer to question 7.
  B ❑ Sabrina, Josie and Amir have different ideas about the answer to question 8.

2 A ❑ The teacher especially made the quiz to have a good time with the class.
  B ❑ The teacher had more than one reason to do the quiz with her class.

3 A ❑ Glasgow is almost as popular for tourists as London.
  B ❑ Edinburgh is more famous for cultural events than Glasgow.

4 A ❑ A muffler is different from a silencer.
  B ❑ A muffler is the same as a silencer.

5 A ❑ Amir mistook the UK for the Commonwealth.
  B ❑ Amir was born in a Commonwealth country.

6 A ❑ The teacher explains the importance of English in the world.
  B ❑ The teacher says English is the most spoken language in the world.

B
THEME
WORDS

3 Choose the correct alternatives

Read *Theme* words on page 96 in your *Textbook*. Circle the correct *Theme* words.

1 A *constitution / society* describes the rights and duties of people in that country.

2 My family lives in Canada but our *roots / customs* are in Australia.

3 Nova has always wanted to become an *explorer / ancestor.*

4 I don't understand what they are saying because they talk *cosmopolitan / gibberish*.

5 It's faster to *communicate / influence* with emails than with letters.

6 The *native language / melting pot* of Canada is French.

7 Adam's distant *inhabitant / ancestor* was a nobleman.

8 You have to show your passport at *customs / constitution*.

9 It's not easy to *reign / influence* Joyce, she has a strong personality.

10 My uncle is a real *melting pot / cosmopolitan*, he has travelled all over the world!

1 b 2 b 3 b 4 a

4 Fill in the words

Fill in the missing *Theme words.*

India

India is the seventh largest country in the world with over one billion **(1)** ________________ That's more than three times the population of the United States although it's three times as small. In India there are seventeen major languages and more than 800 dialects. Hindi is the official language as well as English, so many people are raised **(2)** ________________

India is considered a **(3)** ________________ due to the many different languages and cultural beliefs of people. In the Indian **(4)** ________________, people belong to a certain caste. This is a class system in which you belong to a high(er) or low(er) class. Often, members of higher castes have a greater social status than individuals of a lower caste.

In the 1600s many different countries wanted **(5)** ________________ over India. They wanted **(6)** ________________ expensive goods from India with the rest of the world. Eventually it was the British who made it one of their colonies. In 1947 India became an independent country within the Commonwealth.

Adapted from: indax.com and primaryhomeworkhelp.co.uk

5 Answer the questions

Look at *Jamaica's three languages* on page 97 of your *Textbook*, but don't read the whole text yet. Answer the questions.

Strategy In this exercise you will practise determining a *text's purpose* (tekstdoel). Texts always have a purpose, for instance to inform, instruct, or convince readers. Often the text type already says something about the text's purpose.

1 What kind of text is *Jamaica's three languages*?
A ❑ advertisement B ❑ newspaper article C ❑ review

2 Read the first paragraph. In the first paragraph, the author…
A ❑ gives a summary of the entire text.
B ❑ introduces the topic with an example.
C ❑ presents the main point of the text.

3 Read the other paragraphs. Indicate what the purpose is of each paragraph by drawing lines.

Paragraph 2	confirmation that Jamaica is unique when it comes to languages
Paragraph 3	description of the Lyaric language spoken by Rastafarians
Paragraph 4	description of the two main languages spoken in Jamaica
Paragraph 5	explanation of how the (English) language developed in Jamaica
Paragraph 6	explanation of the importance of a Jamaican singer for Jamaica and the Lyaric language

4 What kind of tone does the text have?
A ❑ positive B ❑ neutral C ❑ negative

5 Read your answers to the previous questions. What do you think is the purpose of the text and why do you think so?

____

6 Complete the sentences

Read *Jamaica's three languages* again. Complete the sentences with the missing information from the text.

1 De eerste alinea bevat een voorbeeld van hoe Jamaicanen ______________________________

2 Jamaican Patois wordt voornamelijk gesproken in ______________________________
en Jamaican English met name in ______________________________

3 Slaven kwamen in aanraking met Engels doordat ______________________________

4 Jamaican Patois bevat invloeden van verschillende andere talen, namelijk ______________________________
____

5 *Lyaric* wordt gesproken door ______________________________

6 Deze groep mensen spreekt Lyaric, omdat ______________________________

7 Bob Marley bekritiseerde ______________________________
en ______________________________

C
READING

8 Bob Marley was belangrijk voor de rastafaribeweging omdat ______

______

7 Solve the puzzle

Read *Jamaica's three languages*. The Dutch words below are all from the text. Translate the words into English and put them in the puzzle. If you do this correctly, you will find another word in the grey boxes.

1 gedeeltelijk ______
2 belangrijk ______
3 ongelijkheid ______
4 gewoon ______
5 informeel ______
6 veroverd ______
7 uitspreken tegen ______
8 verrijkt ______

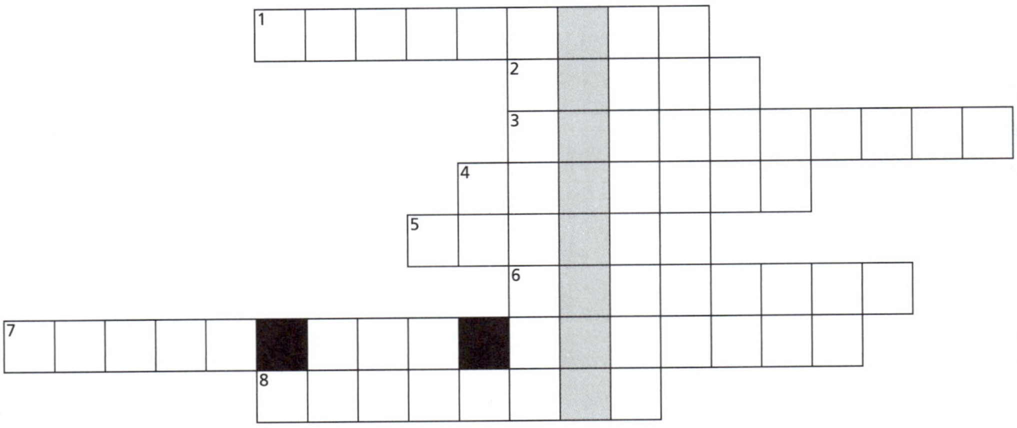

Which word did you find? ______

What does this word mean in Dutch? ______

D
SPEAKING
WRITING

8 Write the sentences

Study *Stone 12* on page 98 of your *Textbook*. Have a look at the pictures. Write a sentence below each picture using the clues in brackets.

(Canada – absoluut – beste plek – genieten – winter)

______
______
______

(ik – vrij zeker – veelgeliefde afhaalmaaltijd – Australië)

______
______
______

(welbekend feit – een van de populairste sporten – dit land)

(iedereen – vertellen – typisch Britse traditie)

(kunt ervan opaan – speciale gelegenheid – kinderen)

(ik geloof – 's werelds grootste – in de Verenigde Staten)

D
SPEAKING
WRITING

9 Complete the dialogue

Complete the dialogue. Use the words in brackets and the *Stone*.

Rick: Hi Melvin. What are you reading?

Melvin: Oh, I'm just browsing through these travel brochures. We're going on a cruise next month. Our first destination is Trinidad and Tobago.

Rick: Trinidad and To... where?

Melvin: Trinidad and Tobago. I'm especially looking forward to visiting Trinidad.
(1) ______________________________ *(dit Caraïbische eiland – staat bekend als – echt carnavalsland)*
(2) ______________________________ *(carnaval – belangrijkste traditie in dit land)*

Rick: So what's it like over there?

Melvin: Well for starters **(3)** ______________________________ *(absoluut – beste plek – genieten – beetje zon)*
The average temperature is 26 degrees Celsius.

Rick: Nice! Then you'd better pack some sunscreen, or you will get burned. Do you know any other interesting facts about the country?

Melvin: Well, being football crazy, this might interest you. Trinidad and Tobago actually qualified for the football World Cup once. That happened in 2006.

Rick: They actually play football there in the tropical heat? You've got to be kidding me. **(4)** ______________________________ *(weet zeker – andere sporten – populairder dan – voetbal)*

Melvin: Well, in this brochure it says that they love playing cricket and football.

Rick: I see. What kind of language do they speak there? **(5)** ______________________________ *(geloof – Spaans – invloedrijkste taal – daar)*

Melvin: Haven't you been paying attention during our history lesson? England used to rule these islands. **(6)** ______________________________ *(alom bekend – Engels – officiële taal)*

Rick: Oh yes, of course. Silly me. Well, it sure sounds like a nice place to visit. I really have to go now. Have fun preparing for your holiday!

Melvin: Okay, I will. Bye!

Now act out the conversation with a classmate.

D
SPEAKING
WRITING

10 Write the blog

You've made a trip to a foreign country. You write down your experiences in a travel blog. You can use your imagination or think about a vacation you've actually been on. You can make things up if there is something you don't know. Use *Stone 12*. Write 80 to 100 words.

Write down:
- which country you visited
- what language(s) they speak
- what kind food the locals eat
- what you liked about the country
- what you disliked about the country

E
GRAMMAR

11 Complete the sentences

Study *Grammar 12* on page 99 of your *Textbook*. Complete the sentences using the words in brackets.

1 Australia is known as the ______ (*large*) island in the world.

2 The cruise to the Carribean turned out ______ (*expensive*) than we had planned.

3 Are the Netherlands really one of the ______ (*little)* corrupt countries in the world?

4 We had a great stay in Dublin. In my opinion, the Irish are the ______ (*friendly*) people ever.

5 The food quality was poor, but the service at the restaurant was even ______ (*bad*).

6 My uncle lives on St Helena which is one of the ______ (*isolated*) places in the world.

7 I think the tour guide we had in London is the ______ (*good*) one we've ever had.

8 There were ______ (*many*) tourists than local residents in the village.

E
GRAMMAR

12 Write the sentences

Write two sentences with the words between brackets. Write one sentence with the comparative (*vergrotende*) form and one sentence with the superlative (*overtreffende*) form. Use the *Grammar*.

Example: *(attractive)* According to this survey the British accent is **more attractive** than the French.
I think Liverpool is one of the **most attractive** cities to live in the UK.

1 (*thin*) ______________________________

____

2 (*beautiful*) ______________________________

____

3 (*noisy*) ______________________________

____

4 (*big*) ______________________________

____

5 (*adventurous*) ______________________________

____

6 (*ill*) ______________________________

____

F
WATCHING

13 Answer the questions

Read the questions carefully. Then watch *English Connection* and answer the questions using keywords. There are no pauses.

1 Rebecca's mother made a joke when Rebecca got the job. What did she say to Rebecca?

____

2 Which two things does she usually tell about the places they visit?

____

3 Why do tourists come to visit Amsterdam according to Rebecca?

____

4 Why do Dutch people often go on a city tour in Amsterdam?

____

5 How does Rebecca treat large groups and small private groups differently?

____

6 How do you discover the best anecdotes about a country according to Rebecca?

____

7 What has Rebecca noticed about the people she guides?

____

14 Draw the pictures

Read *Misunderstandings* on page 100 in your *Textbook*. Then read the misunderstanding below. Draw the story in three pictures to show you know what the misunderstanding is about.

Yesterday I bought a box of dry pet food for our cat and I put it in the kitchen cupboard next to the box of cereals. Early the next morning I went to work. My brother woke up late. He went to the kitchen and took the box. He put a portion in a bowl, put milk over it and ate it. When I came home he told me: ' I didn't like the new cereal.'

15 Fill the gaps

Listen to *Misunderstandings*. There are words missing in the text. They have been replaced by beeps. Tick which of the two words is correct for each beep. There are pauses.

Strategy In this exercise you will practise *gap filling* (het invullen van open plekken in de luistertekst). Listen to the fragment and try to understand all the information.

1	A ❑ But	B ❑ So
2	A ❑ captain	B ❑ coastguard
3	A ❑ also	B ❑ never
4	A ❑ correct	B ❑ wrong
5	A ❑ a mess	B ❑ quiet
6	A ❑ disabled	B ❑ rich
7	A ❑ because of that	B ❑ next to that
8	A ❑ For example	B ❑ So
9	A ❑ an American	B ❑ an Englishman

16 Fill in the mind map

Read the first paragraph of *Irish around the world* on page 100 of your *Textbook*. Answer the questions.

1 What do you think about when Ireland is mentioned? Write down your thoughts and associations in the mind map.

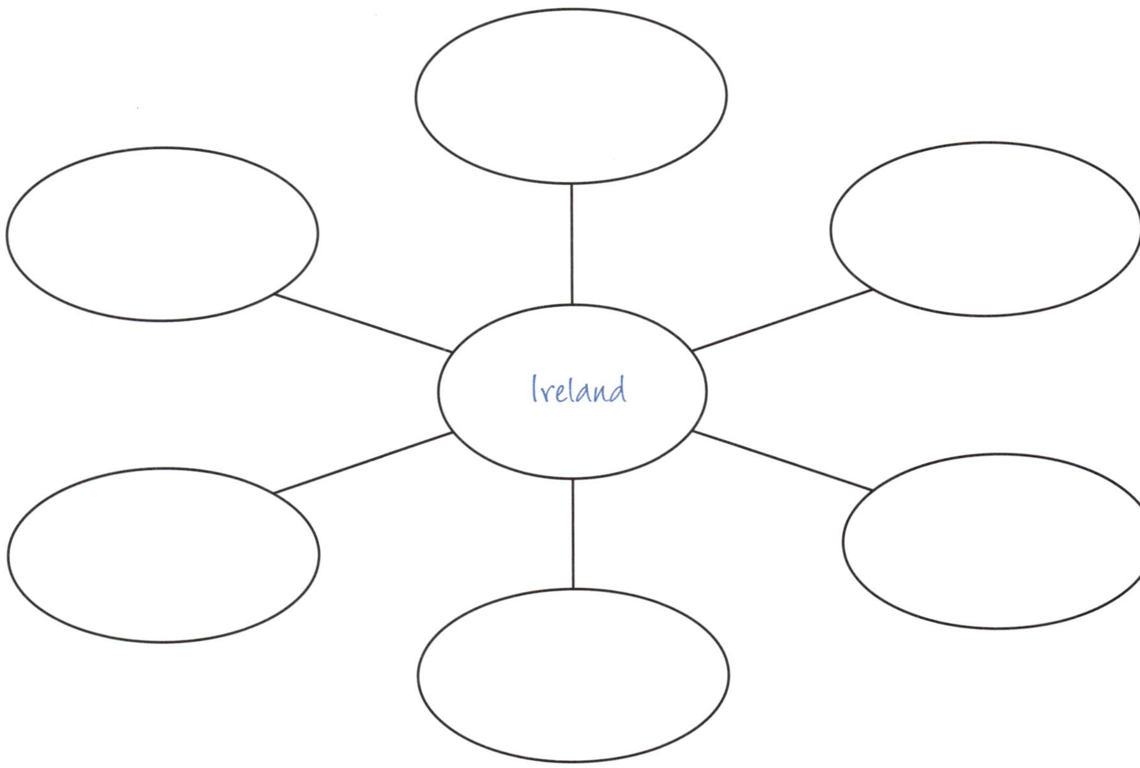

2 What is Ireland well-known for according to the first paragraph?

3 Now read the whole text. Did you find any of the words or expressions from your mind map in the text? If so, which ones?

17 Guess the words

Read *Irish around the world* again and look at the grid on the next page. Find the English words in the text. Guess their meaning and indicate why you think so. Then look up the words in the *Vocabulary* list or in a dictionary.

! **Strategy** In this exercise you will practise tackling *difficult words* (moeilijke woorden). While reading, you sometimes come across difficult words which are needed to understand the text. You can often guess their meaning, for instance because you recognise part of the word, or by carefully reading the context.

Circle:
1 if you already knew the meaning of the word.
2 if you guessed the meaning of the word because you recognise part of it.
3 if you guessed the meaning of the word by reading the sentence(s) around it.

English word	What I think it means...	...and why	What the dictionary says
population (line 7)		*1 / 2 / 3*	
estimated (line 8)		*1 / 2 / 3*	
forebears (line 9)		*1 / 2 / 3*	
presence (line 20)		*1 / 2 / 3*	
seminal (line 36)		*1 / 2 / 3*	
distinctive (line 51)		*1 / 2 / 3*	
to further (line 66)		*1 / 2 / 3*	
considerable (line 73)		*1 / 2 / 3*	

18 Answer the questions

Read *Irish around the world* again. Tick the correct answers or answer the questions in Dutch.

1 What becomes clear about Irish emigration? (paragraph 2)
- A ❑ Australia's population consists for the most part of people of with Irish ancestors.
- B ❑ Most Irish emigrated to Great Britain and Canada.
- C ❑ The USA has the highest number of people of Irish descent.

2 Mention three things that people do on St Patrick's Day.

....

....

3 What can be concluded from paragraph 4?
- A ❑ Irish Folk music was the most popular form of music in the USA for a particular time.
- B ❑ Irish music still makes an impact among people of Irish and non-Irish descent.
- C ❑ The influence of Irish music on American country music is exaggerated.

4 Indicate whether the statements are true or false according to paragraph 5.

		true	false
A	The potato is an important ingredient in the Irish cuisine.	❑	❑
B	Few shops in America sell typically Irish food items.	❑	❑
C	Colcannon is an example of Irish food eaten during celebrations.	❑	❑

5 Which nickname for Ireland is mentioned in the final paragraph?

....

6 Which reason for emigration is NOT mentioned in the final paragraph?
- A ❑ change of climate
- B ❑ economic circumstances
- C ❑ job prospects
- D ❑ study purposes

19 Put in the correct order

Study *Stones 13* and *14* on page 102 of your *Textbook*. Put the words in the correct order and write the sentences. Also write down the Dutch translations.

1 people – to England, – working – abroad – a lot of – has – India – compared

EN ______________________________

NL ______________________________

2 mean – what – sorry, – by – but – I'm – you – do – 'multicultural' – ?

EN ______________________________

NL ______________________________

3 a – sustainable society – than – has – it – become – the past – more – in – our country – was

EN ______________________________

NL ______________________________

4 that – is – a – 'to work like a dog' – very hard' – expression – 'to work – means – common

EN ______________________________

NL ______________________________

5 countries – most – has – other – a – bigger – America – than – population

EN ______________________________

NL ______________________________

6 have – this city – once – changed – was – but – famous – for its – many factories, – times

EN ______________________________

NL ______________________________

20 Complete the forum

Complete the forum by filling in the missing sentences. Use the clues in brackets and the *Stones*.

Back Forward Stop Refresh Home Search Favorites History Mail Print

Agenda | Restaurants | Drinks | Magazines | **Forum**

morrismouse

Posted at 10:16am on April 6

Hail up everyone. I have to write a report about the Commonwealth.

(1) ______________________________ (*weten – helemaal niks – over deze organisatie*)

I also have to write something about one of the countries that are part of the Commonwealth. I think Kenya is an interesting country, but I'm still looking for some nice facts about it.

You would really help me out if you have some interesting information about Kenya or the Commonwealth ;-)

excaliburton *Posted at 11:16am on April 7*

The Commonwealth is a name for countries which were part of the British Empire before they became independent. **(2)** ____________________

____

(*het – vroeger invloedrijk – niet langer het geval*)

There is even such a thing as the Commonwealth Games every four years. It's a bit like the Olympics, but only the 53 nations that are a member can take part of course. **(3)** ____________________

____

(*Commonwealth Games – belangrijk evenement – voor alle landen*)

I hope this info will help you on the way a bit. ;-)

By the way, **(4)** ____________________

____________________ (*wat – bedoel je – 'hail up'?*)

dust2dust *Posted at 8:43am on April 8*

(5) ____________________

__________ (*'hail up' – uitdrukking – 'hello' betekent*), if I'm correct.

(6) ____________________

____________________ (*vaak gebruikt in Jamaica*)

As for your question **@morrismouse**, there are many interesting facts about Kenya.

(7) ____________________

__________ (*dit land – spreken meer talen – dan je zou denken*)

Actually they speak more than 60 languages. Can you imagine that?

Also, **(8)** ____________________

____________________ (*vergelijking met andere Afrikaanse landen – Kenia – veel verschillende soorten dieren*)

That's why thousands of tourists visit the country every year. Maybe you could write about its languages and wildlife? Good luck with your report!

I SPEAKING WRITING

21 Play the role

Work with a classmate. Decide who is pupil A and who is pupil B.

Pupil A Speech card 21
Pupil B Speech card 24

Look up your speech card in *Talking Matters* at the back of your *Activity Book*.

J GRAMMAR

22 Tick the boxes

Study *Grammar 13* on page 103 of your *Textbook*. First underline the *conjunctions* (*voegwoorden*) in the sentences if there are any. Then tick if the sentence is simple (*enkelvoudig*), compound (*samengesteld*) or complex.

	simple	compound	complex
1 Our South Africa trip was perfect although it was rather short.	❑	❑	❑
2 We went to bed early so we could get an early start the next day.	❑	❑	❑
3 We booked a driver to visit the temples for half a day.	❑	❑	❑
4 We hung out in a park nearby, when the tour had ended.	❑	❑	❑
5 Scotland has a lot of mountains and the highest one is Ben Nevis.	❑	❑	❑
6 Rico wants to learn to speak English because his job requires him to.	❑	❑	❑
7 Jamaica once sent a bobsledding team to the Winter Olympics.	❑	❑	❑
8 The city used to be called New Amsterdam but they changed it into New York in 1664.	❑	❑	❑

23 Write down the sentences

Write down logical sentences using the words in the boxes. For each sentence use a different element from each box.

~~*Carol arrived late at work*~~	*although*	*she decided to stay home.*
Lois was really tired	*and*	*we could order a takeaway.*
I could cook	~~*because*~~	~~*she had been in a traffic jam.*~~
Naida went to school	*but*	*he went cycling in the park.*
Jack comes from	*for*	*she felt a bit ill.*
Terry lost his keys	*or*	*he is proud of it.*
	since	
	so	
	when	

1 Carol arrived late at work because she had been in a traffic jam.
2
3
4
5
6

24 Write the sentences

Study *Grammar 14* on page 103 of your *Textbook*. Look at the picture below and describe the situations using relative clauses. Write six sentences. Use the *relative pronouns* (betrekkelijke voornaamwoorden) *who*, *which*, *that* each at least once.

Example: The flag, which has stars on it, is the Australian flag.

1
2
3
4
5
6

J
GRAMMAR

25 Complete the sentences

Complete the sentences. Use *Grammar 14*. If you don't have to use a relative pronoun write down 'X'.

1 I like countries ______________________ have a nice, warm climate.

2 Samuel, ______________________ owns that cool green bike over there, was born in Kenya.

3 I only want to buy a map of the city ______________________ is easy to use and understand.

4 The hotels ______________________ we stayed in were usually quite nice with friendly personnel.

5 I sent an email to my brother ______________________ lives in Pakistan.

6 The Parliament buildings in Ottawa, ______________________ were built in the 19th century, are a popular tourist attraction.

7 The street vendors ______________________ we met in the city centre sold the most delicious snacks.

8 The wild animals, ______________________ didn't look very dangerous at all, were mostly sleeping under trees during our safari trip.

K
WATCHING

26 Answer the questions

Read *The Orient Express!* on page 103 in your *Textbook*. Answer the questions.

1 Are the trains in the Netherlands anything like the Orient Express? Why (not)?

____

____

2 Would you ever want to travel with the Orient Express? Why (not)?

____

____

27 Choose the best alternative

Watch *Orient Express.* Indicate which of the two sentences is true. There are pauses.

! **Strategy** In this exercise you will practise listening globally (*globaal luisteren*). You should try to find out the most important information. You don't have to understand every word.

1 A ❑ De Orient Express is na 1920 langer en groter gemaakt.
B ❑ De Orient Express ziet er nog net zo uit als toen hij is gebouwd.

2 A ❑ Het succes van de Orient Express was te danken aan de boeken van Agatha Christie.
B ❑ Het succes van de Orient Express was te danken aan de snelheid waarmee hij reed.

3 A ❑ De cabines waren voor de tijd waarin de trein gebouwd werd zeer comfortabel.
B ❑ De Orient Express heeft nu veel meer te bieden dan in de twintiger jaren.

4 A ❑ De steward legt uit hoe de alarmknop van de trein werkt.
B ❑ De steward legt uit waarom ze een bepaalde knop hebben aangepast.

Test Yourself ✔

Study the *Vocabulary*, *Grammar*, and *Stones*. Then do the *Test Yourself* below.

You can also do the *Test Yourself* in *Stepping Stones online*. If necessary, it will refer you to extra online exercises to prepare you for the test.

1 Vocabulary

Translate the words into Dutch.

1 cheers ______________________
2 coastguard ______________________
3 cosmopolitan ______________________
4 to emigrate ______________________
5 freezing cold ______________________
6 positive ______________________
7 trainee ______________________
8 tough ______________________

2 Grammar

Fill in the correct form of the adverbs and adjectives.

The Giant Swing and The Blob

Do you like extreme sports and are you into a new challenge? In *Cornwall Super Park* you can find the **(1)** ______________________ (*dangerous*) and the **(2)** ______________________ (*exclusive*) attractions. *The Giant Swing* for example is the **(3)** ______________________ (*high*) swing in the country! It is the **(4)** ______________________ (*scary*) attraction of the park. It's definitely **(5)** ______________________ (*bad*) than any other rollercoaster you know. However, the **(6)** ______________________ (*young*) visitor was a five year old boy! So if he can do it, surely you can!
Another reason to visit the park is *The Blob*: a giant inflatable tube of 3 meters high and 12 meters long. Many people consider this as one of the **(7)** ______________________ (*good*) water attractions in the park.
Why? Because your friend has to sit on one end of the tube, you climb up the **(8)** ______________________ (*big*) tower you've ever seen and then you jump and land on the other side of the tube! Your friend will fly up, and then crash down into the water! Not only hilarious but good for bonding as well! Curious about other activities? Check out the website and watch some of the videos.

Adapted from: adrenalinquarry.co.uk

3 Grammar

Combine the two simple sentences into one complex or compound sentence. Use *and, but, for, nor, or, so, yet, because, since, after, although* or *when.* Sometimes more than one answer is correct.

1 They only visit countries in Great Britain. They don't travel by plane.

____

2 Sammy likes American football. She doesn't know the rules.

____

3 We can go to the beach. Would you like to go to the park?

____

4 I have never been to Las Vegas before. I want to go there sometime.

____

5 My best friend Romeo lives in New York. I don't see him that often.

____

6 Mum said I can watch the film. I've finished doing the dishes.

____

4 Grammar

Complete the sentences.

1 This travel guide, ______________ I bought yesterday, has a lot of information about Pakistan's most beautiful sights.

2 Jennifer, the girl ______________ I met last summer, is coming to visit me next week.

3 Barbados, ______________ lies in the Caribbean Sea, used to be a British colony.

4 The dog, ______________ lived on the streets in India, was brought to an animal shelter.

5 I bought the watch ______________ I'm wearing from a vendor in Malta.

6 Susy organised a surprise party for her friends, ______________ come from all over the world.

7 The charity ______________ I support, has over three thousand subscribers.

8 We are going to travel to Australia, ________ is going to be a great experience.

5 Stones

Make the correct combinations. Then translate the sentences into Dutch.

It used to be a poor country	what you're talking about.
We all know that English	It is an important part of Irish culture.
I'm certain that they speak	a more multicultural society than it was in the past.
Scotland has more	three languages in this country.
I'm sorry but I don't understand	but it no longer is.
What is Saint Patrick's Day?	is the official language in Jamaica.
England has become	bring a small gift when you're invited for dinner.
It's quite common in this country to	lakes than you might think.

1 EN ______________________________

NE ______________________________

2 EN ______________________________

NE ______________________________

3 EN ______________________________

NE ______________________________

4 EN ______________________________

NE ______________________________

5 EN ______________________________

NE ______________________________

6 EN ______________________________

NE ______________________________

7 EN ______________________________

NE ______________________________

8 EN ______________________________

NE ______________________________

	OK!	Herhaling (bladzijde 56-60)
Vocabulary	❏ 0-3 ft	❏ meer dan 3 ft → opdracht 7, 8
Grammar	❏ 0-7 ft	❏ meer dan 7 ft → opdracht 9, 10, 11
Stones	❏ 0-3 ft	❏ meer dan 3 ft → opdracht 12, 13, 14

Let hierbij ook goed op je spelling!

Heb je overal OK aangekruist? Ga dan naar *Verrijking* op bladzijde 61.

Task

>> TASKCARD

My videolog
Je gaat een vlog opnemen voor een uitwisseling.

Taalportfolio
A2 Ik kan in eenvoudige beschrijvende taal vergelijkingen maken tussen en korte uitspraken doen over dingen en bezittingen.
A2 Ik kan alledaagse aspecten beschrijven van mijn omgeving.

ERK

STEP 1

Preparation

Look at the *Task* on page 104 of your *Textbook*. In this *Task* you are going to record a vlog for an exchange student.

- Study *Stones 12*, *13* and *14* on pages 98 and 102 of your *Textbook*.
- Learn the words from the *Vocabulary* on pages 105 to 107 of your *Textbook*.

! **Tip** First read the sentences under *Step 4: Evaluation* on page 50. Keep these points in mind when doing your *Task*.

STEP 2

Orientation

Read the text on page 104 of your *Textbook* and answer the following questions in English.

1 To whom is the text addressed and where does the person come from?

______

______

2 What is the purpose of the text?

______

______

3 If you had to tell a foreigner about your town or city, which things would you mention?

______

______

______

STEP 3

Realisation

1 You are going to make a vlog for someone from an English-speaking country who is coming to your town or city for a school exchange. First decide which country he or she is coming from and then fill in the fact file using key words. You can look up information online.

FACT FILE	
COUNTRY	
CAPITAL	
TRADITIONS/CELEBRATIONS	
CLIMATE	
POPULATION	
POPULAR SPORTS	

2 Now fill in the fact file for your own city or town. Use key words.

FACT FILE	
COUNTRY	
CAPITAL	
TRADITIONS/CELEBRATIONS	
CLIMATE	
POPULATION	
POPULAR SPORTS	
OTHER INTERESTING INFO	

3 Record your vlog (for example on your smartphone) with the help of your classmate. Use the fact files that you made in question 2.

Make sure you:
– give interesting information about your country and hometown.
– compare traditions/celebrations from your country with those of the exchange student.
– make your vlog interesting to look at. For example, you could show some typical local attractions or products from your city/town.

Your video should take between 3 and 4 minutes.

4 Work together with three or four classmates. Take turns showing your vlog. When watching a vlog, write down your opinion of it. Use the schedule below to do this.

Checklist vlog			
Name classmate			
He/She uses clear language.	–	+/–	+
He/She speaks at a good pace.	–	+/–	+
He/She gives information about his her hometown.	–	+/–	+
He/She makes comparisons between his her hometown and country of exchange student.	–	+/–	+
He/She uses extra material to make the vlog interesting to look at.	–	+/–	+

After all the vlogs have been shown, take turns to give your opinion, in English, on each vlog.

STEP 4

Evaluation

Together with a classmate, talk about the vlogs that you made. Indicate whether each sentence is *true* or *false*.

	true	**false**
I used words from the *Vocabulary*.	❑	❑
I used words and sentences from the *Stones*.	❑	❑
I talked about the differences between my hometown and a foreign country.	❑	❑
I gave my opinion about my classmates' vlogs.	❑	❑

Keep (a copy of) your vlog in your language portfolio.

Herhaling & Verrijking

Theme 4 Can you believe it?

	Activity Book ex.
Herhaling	
Vocabulary	
Vocabulaire	*1, 2*
Grammar	
10 Summary of the tenses *(samenvatting werkwoordstijden)*	*3*
11 'If' sentences	*4*
Stones	
10 Finding out how things work	*5*
11 Making predictions	*6*
Verrijking	
The power of the placebo	*1, 2*

Theme 5 English around the world

	Activity Book ex.
Herhaling	
Vocabulary	
Vocabulaire	*7, 8*
Grammar	
12 Comparatives and superlatives *(trappen van vergelijking)*	*9*
13 Complex and compound sentences *(samengestelde en complexe zinnen)*	*10*
14 Relative clauses *(betrekkelijke bijzinnen)*	*11*
Stones	
12 Talking about facts and convictions	*12*
13 Making comparisons	*13*
14 Asking for and giving clarification	*14*
Verrijking	
Life in Singapore	*3, 4*

1 Vocabulary

Study the *Vocabulary* of *Theme 4* on pages 91 to 93 of your *Textbook*. Fill in the English translation of the words in the puzzle.

1 rekenen
2 kennis
3 tientallen
4 verwerken
5 beheersen
6 vervangen
7 uitpakken
8 bedrog

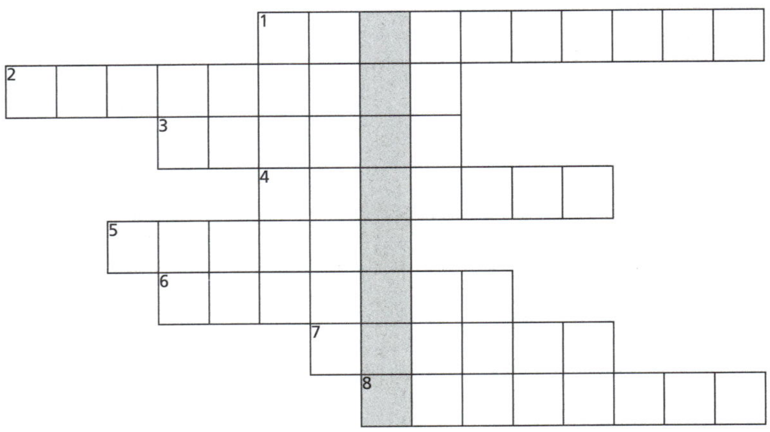

Which word do you read in the grey boxes? ____________________

What is the Dutch translation of this word? ____________________

2 Vocabulary

Study the *Vocabulary* of *Theme 4* again. Circle the incorrect word in the sentence. Then write down the word that would best replace it behind the sentence.

aim – coincidence – excessively – negotiate – observe – obvious – physics – sign up

1 You have to fix for this photography course. ____________________
2 Capacity is my favourite subject at school. ____________________
3 I always refer the birds in our garden. ____________________
4 It was a permission that my cousin stayed at the same hotel. ____________________
5 It's curious that he can't finish this job. ____________________
6 The parties had to conduct with each other in order to reach an agreement. ____________________
7 What is the stack of this research project? ____________________
8 He works out merely in the gym every day. ____________________

For more *Vocabulary* practice go to *Stepping Stones online*.

HERHALING THEME 4

3 Grammar 10

Study Grammar 10 on page 85 of your *Textbook*. Fill in the right tense in the sentence. Use the verbs from the box.

to ask – to eat – to learn – to live – to play – to phone – to watch – to write

1 At the moment he ______________________ a new book.
2 My brother ______________________ TV in his room all day.
3 I ______________________ my teacher for help with these difficult sums.
4 We ______________ never ______________ any Mexican dishes before.
5 Most people ______________________ to swim when they are young.
6 I ______________________ you back this evening. I promise.
7 My dog ______________________ in the park yesterday.
8 We ______________________ in Brighton for eight years now.

4 Grammar 11

Study *Grammar* 11 on page 89 of your Textbook. Complete the email by using the clues in brackets.

Send Quote Address Attach Options Spelling Save Security Stop

To: liban@email.com
Subject: cool trick

Hi Liban,

Yesterday I told you and Mike that **(1)** ______________________ (*als ik tijd had – uitvinden hoe truc werkt*) that we saw in town last weekend. Well, I had a look on the internet and it didn't take long to find it. I found a video on YouTube in which the trick is explained step by step. **(2)** ______________________ (*als volgen instructies – makkelijk om truc uit te voeren*). I know how busy you are today but **(3)** ______________________ (*als je tijd hebt – bekijk video*) in which everything is explained. Why don't you try the trick on your brother and sister, I'll do the same this afternoon. **(4)** ______________________ (*als alles goed gaat – kunnen truc morgen in de klas doen).* I've also promised Peter to let him know how the trick works, but I can't seem to find his email address. You've got it, haven't you? I **(5)** ______________ (*stuur hem – link video – als jij zijn adres geeft).* So, let me know how you get on with the trick and I'll see you tomorrow at school.

Bye,
Nathan

For more *Grammar* practice go to *Stepping Stones online*.

5 Stone 10

Study *Stone 10* on page 84 of your Textbook. Write down a correct sentence. Use the phrases in the boxes.

I wanted to find	*how people learn best?*	*Paul says he can learn better in*
to remember the name carefully.	*I asked some students to*	*How can you determine*
fill in an observation form.	*the library.*	*out how this trick works.*
The man asked me	*people concentrate best*	*How can you figure out how*

1 ______

2 ______

3 ______

4 ______

5 ______

6 ______

6 Stone 11

Study *Stone 11* on page 88 of your Textbook. Write down what you say in English.

1 In de volgende eeuw zullen we in staat zijn tientallen talen te spreken.

______

2 Wij geloven dat alle leraren over 50 jaar een digitale leeromgeving zullen gebruiken in de klas.

______

3 Als je genoeg slaap krijgt, zal het gemakkelijker zijn om te studeren.

______

4 Wij verwachten dat spellen die je hersenen trainen populairder zullen worden.

______

5 Onderzoeken wijzen uit dat over twintig jaar niemand het internet meer zal gebruiken.

______

For more *Stones* practice go to *Stepping Stones online*.

7 Vocabulary

Study the *Vocabulary of Theme 5* on pages 105 to 107 of your *Textbook*.
The letters of the words are mixed up. First write down the English word.
Then write the Dutch translation.

	English	Dutch
1 csanetro	………………	………………
2 teninlyse	………………	………………
3 alusac	………………	………………
4 lopdevemetn	………………	………………
5 gralene	………………	………………
6 cumutillaltur	………………	………………
7 evitisop	………………	………………
8 ot edceru	………………	………………

8 Vocabulary

Complete the text with the words from the box.

associated with – bilingual – densely populated – formerly – frequently – inhabitant – major – to trade

Introducing Malta

Malta, **(1)** ……………… a British colony, offers many prehistoric temples, cliffs, hidden coves, thrilling scuba diving and remarkable history. Tourism plays a **(2)** ……………… role in this country, which is an island located in the Mediterranean Sea, just 80 kilometres south of Italy. It is one of the world's smallest and most **(3)** ……………… countries. Malta is still **(4)** ……………… Great Britain because they are a member of the Commonwealth. Nearly every **(5)** ……………… of Malta is **(6)** ………………; they speak English as well as Maltese. These are the two official languages of Malta. However, Italian is also **(7)** ……………… spoken, because many Maltese businesses **(8)** ……………… with Italy.

For more *Vocabulary* practice go to *Stepping Stones online*.

9 Grammar 12

Study *Grammar 12* on page 99 of your *Textbook*. Look at the illustrations and write sentences. Use *comparatives* and *superlatives*.

1 (*Mexico – warm land*) ______________________

2 (*Costa Rica – warmer – Mexico*) ______________________

3 (*warmste land – Egypte*) ______________________

4 (*Noki-telefoon – goedkoop*) ______________________

5 (*HTS-telefoon – goedkoper – Noki-telefoon*) ______________________

6 (*Leno-telefoon – goedkoopste*) ______________________

7 (*Dave – weinig*) ______________________

8 (*Josie – minder – Dave*) ______________________

9 (*Tom – minste*) ______________________

10 Grammar 13

Study *Grammar 13* on page 103 of your *Textbook*. Choose the correct alternative in the sentence.

1 You can buy a new laptop *because / or* you can buy a new tablet.

2 I used to play badminton every day, *but / nor* now I never play anymore.

3 *Since / When* my mother was young, she was a ballet dancer.

4 I don't like sightseeing, *although / for* I enjoyed visiting the Taj Mahal.

5 We are going on holiday to England *and / yet* Wales.

6 Shirley did a project on bilingual children, *so / yet* she knows a lot about this subject.

7 I won't go to the concert, *because / but* I don't like rock music.

8 *After / Although* I have finished cooking, I'll help you do your homework.

11 Grammar 14

Study *Grammar 14* on page 103 of your *Textbook*. Make one sentence from the two sentences by using a relative clause.

1 My father is very smart. He speaks six languages.

My father, who is very smart, speaks six languages.

2 This bird can't fly. It only lives in New Zealand.

3 John is my best friend. He plays in a band.

4 This computer is second-hand. It broke down yesterday.

5 This house was sold last week. It is very old.

6 My brother is three years older than me. He has passed his exams.

For more *Grammar* practice go to *Stepping Stones online*.

12 Stone 12

Study Stone 12 on page 98 of your *Textbook*. Complete the dialogue using the clues.

Ella: Hi Janet? How are you getting on with your presentation on Canada?

Janet: Great! But there's so much to tell that I've decided to focus on three subjects only; language, sports and music.

Ella: What's there to tell about the language? **(1)** ______

(*We weten allemaal dat Engels de officiële taal van Canada is*)

Janet: And that's where you're wrong! Canada has two official languages: French and English.

Ella: I didn't know! Oh well, **(2)** ______

(*Ik ben ervan overtuigd dat Engels de invloedrijkste taal van Canada is*)

Everything you always hear about Canada is in English isn't it?

Janet: Just wait for my presentation and I'll tell you all about it.

Ella: So, what about sports in Canada? **(3)** ______

(*Het is alom bekend dat ijshockey de meest populaire sport in Canada is*)

Janet: You're certainly right about that. I'm going to talk about some of Canada's ice hockey successes and you'll see some spectacular videos.

Ella: That sounds great. Then you've still got music to talk about. Why music? I don't even know any Canadian singers.

Janet: You don't know Justin Bieber and Michael Bublé? **(4)** ______________________________

____

(Canada is absoluut een goede plaats om van popmuziek te genieten)

Ella: I certainly didn't know they were Canadian. Well, I guess **(5)** ______________________________

____

(Canada staat bekend als een land met interessante culturen)

I'm looking forward to your presentation.

13 Stone 13

Study *Stone 13* on page 102 of your *Textbook*. Answer the questions.

1 Does Australia have a lot of coastline?

(Australië – meer kustlijn – dan – meeste – andere landen)

____

____

2 Does Poland have a lot of people working abroad?

(in vergelijking met – Duitsland – Polen – weinig mensen – in buitenland – werken)

____

____

3 Is the USA densely populated?

(VS – geworden – dichter bevolkt – dan – vroeger – was)

____

____

4 What was Ireland known for in the past?

(Ierland – vroeger – bekend – door – textielindustrie – maar – tijden – veranderd)

____

____

5 What did this country use to be like?

(ooit – arm – land – maar – nu niet meer)

____

____

14 Stone 14

Study *Stone 14* on page 102 of your *Textbook.* Write the sentence by putting the words in the correct order. Then translate the sentences.

1 'goodbye' – that means – a common – 'cheers' – is – expression – 'thank you' – or –

EN ______________________________

NL ______________________________

2 you're – sorry – but – I – understand – what – saying – don't – I'm

EN ______________________________

NL ______________________________

3 part – it – important – of – Scottish – culture – is – an

EN ______________________________

NL ______________________________

4 do – mean – you – what – by – that – proverb – ?

EN ______________________________

NL ______________________________

5 hasn't – Miley – the – slightest – idea – got

EN ______________________________

NL ______________________________

For more *Stones* practice go to *Stepping Stones online*.

VERRIJKING
THEME 4

1 Write the sentences

Read *The power of the placebo* on page 110 of your *Textbook*. Write down the first two words and the last two words of the sentence or phrase that gives the following information.

1 Veel testen laten zien dat placebo's vaak net zo goed werken als echte medicijnen.

2 Het placebo had een positief effect op hun migraine.

3 Door het veranderen van de naam op de envelop werkte het placebo net zo goed als het echte medicijn.

4 Deelnemers weten vaak niet of ze een echt medicijn of een placebo slikken.

5 Er doen verschillende verklaringen de ronde over het sterker worden van het placebo-effect.

6 Tot nu toe is er geen duidelijke verklaring voor het toenemen van het placebo effect.

2 Answer the questions

Read *The power of the placebo* again. Answer the questions in English.

1 What has become clear from the research of drugs and placebos?

2 Who were the participants of the experiment at Harvard medical School?

3 According to the text, how can you prove if placebos work? Explain your answer.

4 What two things does the FDA ask before a new drug is put on the market?

5 Why is the pharmaceutical industry worried about the strong placebo response?

6 How can a member of the research team influence the outcome of the trial?

7 What do they have to do in order to explain the rise of the placebo effect?

8 Explain the title of the text in your own words.

VERRIJKING THEME 5

3 Fact file

Read *Life in Singapore* on page 111 of your *Textbook*. Complete the fact file with information from the text.

FACT FILE	SINGAPORE
SIZE	
POPULATION	
OFFICIAL LANGUAGES	
NICKNAME	
CRIME RATE	
WEATHER	
COST PUBLIC TRANSPORT	

4 Choose the correct answer

Read *Life in Singapore again.* Choose the correct answer.

1 What does the text say about the population of Singapore?
A ❑ Half of it consists of foreigners.
B ❑ Part of it consists of foreigners.

2 What is said about Singlish?
A ❑ It is spoken in formal situations.
B ❑ It is spoken in informal situations.

3 If you throw an empty bottle on the streets, what usually happens?
A ❑ You have to clean up the streets.
B ❑ You have to pay a fine.

4 What does Jonathan say about spending leisure time?
A ❑ He prefers going to cheap places like Luge and Adventure Cove Waterpark.
B ❑ He advises to use the internet to get some more tips.

5 What does the text say about crime?
A ❑ There isn't a lot of crime, but it's not safe to go out late at night.
B ❑ There isn't a lot of crime, so you can go out day and night.

6 What does Jonathan mention about expats with regards to his social life?
A ❑ He finds it hard to see his expat friends leaving the country.
B ❑ The large population of expats provide a good opportunity to make new friends.

7 Why is the weather called 'intense'?
A ❑ It takes a lot of time to get adjusted to such extreme temperatures.
B ❑ Most of the time it's extremely hot or extremely wet.

8 What does the text say about transport in Singapore?
A ❑ It's cheap and it gets you anywhere.
B ❑ It's cheap but often slow because of other traffic.

TABLE OF CONTENTS

Exam Preparation

In de *Exam Preparation* ga je je voorbereiden op het examen. Je gaat oefenen met vragen en opdrachten zoals je die in het schoolexamen en het Centraal Schriftelijk Examen (CSE) zult tegenkomen. De *Exam Preparation* bestaat uit vijf onderdelen: *Listening*, *Watching*, *Reading*, *Writing* en *Speaking*.
Bij *Listening* en *Watching* oefen je met het toepassen van strategieën. Die zullen je tijdens het examen helpen om de vragen te beantwoorden. Bij *Reading* oefen je met de verschillende vraagtypes die je tegen kunt komen tijdens het Centraal Schriftelijk Examen. Je maakt eerst steeds een aantal opdrachten die je voorbereiden op de vragen uit het CSE of het kijk- en luisterexamen. Daarna maak je de vragen zelf. De antwoorden op al deze vragen kun je controleren op pagina 74 van je *Activity Book*.
Bij *Speaking* en *Writing* oefen je met verschillende schrijf- en spreekopdrachten die je tijdens je schoolexamen kunt tegenkomen.

13 LISTENING

In dit onderdeel ga je oefenen met vragen die je tijdens het kijk- en luisterexamen tegen kunt komen. Dit examen bevat een lang luisterfragment dat bestaat uit twee delen. Meestal begint het fragment met een interview, daarna volgt een aantal korte nieuwsberichten. Naast de luisterfragmenten bevat het examen ook een videofragment. Om de vragen bij de fragmenten goed te beantwoorden, kun je verschillende kijk- en luisterstrategieën inzetten. Hieronder oefen je met het toepassen van deze strategieën.

! **Tip** In het Cito Kijk- en luisterexamen is er na iedere vraag 10 seconden tijd om de vraag te beantwoorden én de volgende vraag te lezen.

1 Strategieopdracht

1 Bij deze en de volgende opdracht ga je luisteren naar een interview. Lees *Skydiving* op bladzijde 67 van je *Textbook*. Beantwoord de vraag.

De persoon die hier aan het woord is, vindt skydiven ______

Dit weet ik omdat hij de woorden ______ en

______ gebruikt.

2 Lees de examenvraag hieronder. Je moet daarbij *intensief luisteren*. Welke woorden vallen op en waar moet je dus vooral op letten bij het intensief luisteren?

______

3 Luister nu naar de inleiding van *Skydiving* en kruis het juiste antwoord aan.

Waarop wijst Ian Lewis hier vooral?

A ❑ wat voor mensen skydiven
B ❑ hoe bijzonder skydiven is
C ❑ de moeilijkheid van zijn beroep

Controleer je antwoorden op bladzijde 74 van je *Activity Book*.

13
LISTENING

2 Cito voorbereidingsvragen

Listen to *Skydiving* and choose the correct alternatives. There is a pause after each question.

1 Hoe beschrijft Ian skydiven?
A ❑ Het zijn de gekke stunts die worden uitgevoerd tijdens de val.
B ❑ Het is de val uit het vliegtuig tot het moment dat de parachute opengaat.
C ❑ Het is de sprong uit het vliegtuig tot en met de landing.

2 Welk aspect benadrukt Ian hier?
A ❑ dat de meeste skydivers uit een bepaald sociaal milieu komen
B ❑ aan welke eisen je moet voldoen als je wilt gaan skydiven
C ❑ waarom iedere skydiver eerst een gezondheidstest moet doen

3 Wat zegt Ian over de risico's van skydiven?
A ❑ Die moet je zeker niet onderschatten.
B ❑ Die zijn er, maar in zeer beperkte mate.
C ❑ Die zijn er vooral voor de wat oudere skydivers.

4 Waarop wijst Ian met betrekking tot de hoogte van waar gesprongen wordt?
A ❑ Die hangt af van de bekwaamheid en ervaring van de skydivers.
B ❑ Die wordt vaak lager naarmate skydivers meer ervaring hebben.
C ❑ Die mag in alle gevallen door de skydivers zelf worden bepaald.

5 Wat zegt Ian over het gevoel tijdens skydiven?
A ❑ Het voelt soms alsof je in een achtbaan zit.
B ❑ Het is verslavend en voelt als echt vliegen.
C ❑ Het gevoel is afhankelijk van de hoogte vanwaar je springt.

6 Wat beschrijft Ian hier?
A ❑ dat het risico van een parachute die niet werkt zeer klein is
B ❑ waarom sommige skydivers soms twee parachutes opentrekken
C ❑ het verschil tussen de eerste en de tweede parachute

7 Over welk aspect van het skydiven praat Ian hier?
A ❑ dat je meerdere manieren van vallen moet hebben uitgeprobeerd
B ❑ dat het trainen in windtunnels een verplicht onderdeel is
C ❑ dat je mentaal goed voorbereid moet zijn op skydiven

8 Waarop wijst Ian hier?
A ❑ dat zijn broer hem heeft geleerd hoe je het beste kunt springen
B ❑ dat hij zijn aanvankelijke angst snel heeft overwonnen
C ❑ dat hij begrijpt waarom mensen bang zijn om te gaan skydiven

3 Strategieopdracht

1 Bij deze en de volgende opdracht ga je luisteren naar een aantal kort berichten. Daarbij moet je gericht luisteren. Lees de vragen bij 2 van deze opdracht door. Bekijk de verschillen in de antwoorden. Op welke Engelse woorden moet je tijdens het luisteren letten?

Op de woorden ______________________________

2 Luister nu naar het eerste bericht. Wat wordt er in dit bericht verteld over een hagedis?
A ❑ Die werd door een klas geadopteerd, nadat hij was gevonden in een salade.
B ❑ Die werd op een school gebruikt om experimenten mee te doen.
C ❑ Die werd in de vrije natuur losgelaten, nadat hij weer op temperatuur was.

13 LISTENING

3 Welke delen van de luistertekst geven het juiste antwoord van de vorige vraag aan?
   A ❑ *...a tiny green lizard found by a New Jersey kindergarten... adopted it as a mascot.*
   B ❑ *...Warmth restore its energy and soon the lizard was on its way to Riverside Elementary School.*
   C ❑ *...The lizard lurking in the salad has turned out to be a valuable learning experience.*

Controleer je antwoorden op bladzijde 74 van je van je *Activity Book*.

4 Cito voorbereidingvragen

Now listen to the news items and choose the correct alternatives. There is a pause after each question.

1 Waarover gaat dit bericht?
   A ❑ Over een jongen die probeerde gestolen geld te verbergen door het in een rivier te gooien.
   B ❑ Over een jongen die geld had gevonden in een rivier en nu een deel daarvan opeist.
   C ❑ Over een dief die meende na een jaar recht te hebben op geld dat hij gestolen had.

2 Wat gaat er gebeuren met het skelet van een dinosaurus?
   A ❑ Dat blijft nog zes maanden in Londen, waarna het een nieuwe vaste plek krijgt.
   B ❑ Dat zal op verschillende plekken in het land voor het publiek te zien zijn.
   C ❑ Het zal worden tentoongesteld naast het skelet van een blauwe walvis.

3 Wat blijkt uit dit bericht over een uil in Oregon?
   A ❑ Die is, na mensen te hebben belaagd, door de politie gevangen.
   B ❑ Die heeft een politieman vrij ernstig gewond door hem aan te vallen.
   C ❑ Die levert veel gevaar door regelmatig mensen aan te vallen.

4 Welk voorval vond er plaats op het vliegveld van Denver?
   A ❑ Een man verstoorde op illegale wijze een reünie van vliegtuigpersoneel.
   B ❑ Een man hield zijn vliegtuig op door op de alarmknop te drukken.
   C ❑ Een man wilde op illegale wijze aan boord van een vliegtuig zien te komen.

5 Wat wordt er gezegd in dit bericht over een man in een rolstoel?
   A ❑ Hij ontkwam nadat hij een ongewapende bankoverval had gepleegd.
   B ❑ Hij pleegde al voor de zoveelste maal een gewapende overval.
   C ❑ Hij stond bekend om zijn kenmerkende manier van overvallen.

6 Wat wordt er hier over de hond Estrella gezegd?
   A ❑ Ze heeft veel hinder van het feit dat ze twee van haar poten mist.
   B ❑ Ze is erg populair bij veel mensen als gevolg van haar handicap.
   C ❑ Ze speelt veel met een kangoeroe die in dezelfde opvang leeft.

14 WATCHING

1 Strategieopdracht

1 Lees *The Paralympics* op bladzijde 67 van je *Textbook*. Vul de fact file in.

FACT FILE	PARALYMPIC SKIING
ONDERDEEL VAN	
TWEE PARALYMPIC SKI-ONDERDELEN	
AFSTANDEN	
TWEE SOORTEN BEPERKINGEN	

2 Je gaat oefenen met *intensief kijken en luisteren.* Lees vraag 3 van deze opdracht en de Cito-voorbereidingsvragen in opdracht 4 hieronder door. Welke van de onderstaande aspecten komen in het kijkfragment vooral aan de orde? Kruis aan waarover je verwacht iets te gaan horen.
- ❑ de oprichting en het ontstaan van de Paralympische Spelen
- ❑ tegenstanders van het organiseren van de Paralympische Spelen
- ❑ hoe moeilijk het is om als gehandicapte aan intensieve sport te doen
- ❑ de enorme kosten die de Paralympische Spelen met zich meebrengen
- ❑ de technische hulpmiddelen die beschikbaar zijn voor paralympische sporters

3 Bekijk nu het eerste gedeelte van *The Paralympics.* Kruis het juiste antwoord aan. Wat wordt hier duidelijk gemaakt over Sir Ludwig Guttman?
A ❑ Hij heeft veel betekend voor mensen met rugproblemen.
B ❑ Hij raakte ernstig gewond na een auto-ongeluk.
C ❑ Hij werd in de oorlog opgepakt door de Duitsers.

Controleer je antwoorden op bladzijde 74 van je *Activity Book*.

2 Cito-voorbereidingsvragen

Watch *The Paralympics* and choose the correct answers. There are pauses.

Eerste deel: Dr Guttmann

1 Waarop wijst Philip Lewis hier?
A ❑ dat hij aanvankelijk door Dr Guttmann werd weggestuurd
B ❑ hoe Dr Guttmann zich opstelde tegenover zijn patiënten
C ❑ in welke aandoeningen Dr Guttmann gespecialiseerd was

2 Wat komt hier naar voren als het belangrijkste in de behandeling van Dr Guttmann?
A ❑ complicaties meteen behandelen
B ❑ het geloof in volledig herstel
C ❑ voldoende beweging

3 Wat wordt in dit fragment duidelijk gemaakt?
A ❑ Guttmann had een belangrijke rol bij het ontstaan van de Paralympische Spelen.
B ❑ In 1952 werden de bestaande spelen omgedoopt in de 'Paralympische Spelen'.
C ❑ Aan de eerste Paralympische Spelen deden ook gezonde sporters mee.

Tweede deel: Tim Farr: British Paralympic skier

4 Wat wordt hier duidelijk over Tim Farr?
A ❑ dat hij denkt ooit weer te kunnen lopen
B ❑ dat hij zich terugvocht binnen zijn geliefde sport
C ❑ dat hij somber was nadat hij zijn rug had gebroken

5 Welk aspect van Tim wordt hier vooral belicht?
A ❑ hoe goed hij was in zijn sport
B ❑ hoe hij er op foto's van vroeger uitziet
C ❑ hoe optimistisch hij in het leven staat

Derde deel: Tom Aggar: Paralympic rower

6 Wat wordt er in dit fragment duidelijk gemaakt over Tom Aggar?
A ❑ in welke soorten boten en teams hij roeit
B ❑ op welke manier hij roeit en hoe zijn boot is aangepast
C ❑ waarom hij roeien zoveel leuker vindt dan zijn eerdere sport, rugby

7 Wat zegt Tom over het meedoen aan de Paralympische Spelen?
A ❑ Hij vindt het trainen voor de spelen behoorlijk zwaar.
B ❑ Hij wist van tevoren dat hij de spelen in 2008 ging winnen.
C ❑ Hij heeft het hoogst haalbare erin bereikt.

Vierde deel: Paralympic gadgets

8 Waarover gaat dit fragment vooral?
A ❑ over gehandicapte studenten die aan sport willen doen
B ❑ over technologische uitvindingen voor de gehandicaptensport
C ❑ over het motiveren van gehandicapten om aan sport te doen

15 READING

In dit onderdeel ga je oefenen met vragen die je tijdens het Centraal Schriftelijk Examen tegen kunt komen. Dit examen bevat meerdere (soorten) teksten met verschillende soorten vragen. Om de vragen bij de teksten goed te beantwoorden, kun je verschillende leesstrategieën inzetten. Hieronder oefen je met het toepassen van deze strategieën op de verschillende vraagtypes.

! **Let op!** Beantwoord een *open vraag* altijd in het Nederlands, behalve als het anders is aangegeven.

1 Meerkeuzevragen

Bij deze en de volgende opdracht ga je oefenen met het beantwoorden van *meerkeuzevragen.* Lees de uitleg over meerkeuzevragen in *Exam Help* op bladzijde 155 van je *Textbook*. Vink de juiste zinnen aan.

❑ Het is belangrijk om eerst te achterhalen wat voor een tekst je gaat lezen.

❑ Het is nuttig om van tevoren de vraag en de bijbehorende antwoorden te lezen.

❑ Probeer altijd eerst zelf een antwoord te formuleren op de gestelde vraag.

❑ *Skimmen* is hetzelfde als iets heel nauwkeurig lezen.

❑ Voor het beantwoorden van vragen bij korte(re) teksten moet je vaak zoekend lezen.

Controleer je antwoorden op bladzijde 74 van je *Activity Book*.

2 Examenvraag

Lees *Adventure playgrounds* op bladzijde 68 van je *Textbook*. Beantwoord daarna de examenvragen.

1 What is said about adventure playgrounds in paragraph 1? (*1p*)
A ❑ They are designed to look like computer games.
B ❑ They are often too dangerous and need to become safer.
C ❑ They can help youngsters learn about making the right choices.
D ❑ They will become information centres to educate teenagers.

2 Which educational change is part of Ed Balls' plan, according to paragraph 2? (*1p*)
He wants schools to...
A ❑ find placements for pupils after their finals.
B ❑ pay more attention to the home situation of pupils.
C ❑ set apart unruly pupils in special classrooms.
D ❑ teach more pupils individually or in small groups.

16 READING

1 Moeilijke woorden

Read *Jellyfish shut down Swedish nuclear reactor* on page 000 of your *Textbook*. Below are some keywords from the text. Match the words with their meaning. Draw lines. Under 'meaning' two words will be left over. Use a dictionary if necessary.

Look at *Exam Help* on page 155 in your *Textbook* under *Algemene tips* what it says about using your dictionary.

Words	Meaning
	spuug
shut down	oppervlaktes
clog	verstoppen
clear	onder water zetten
flood	afbreken
gob	uitschakelen
bodies	schoonmaken
	lichamen

Controleer je antwoorden op bladzijde 74 van je *Activity Book*.

2 Exam Question

Read *Jellyfish shut down Swedish nuclear reactor* on page 69 of your Textbook. Answer the exam question.

1 'Jellyfish shut down Swedish nuclear reactor' (titel)
Hoe hebben kwallen dit veroorzaakt? (*1p*)

Ze veroorzaakten...
A ❑ een vastgelopen reactormotor.
B ❑ lekkage in het koelwatersysteem.
C ❑ verstopping in de toevoerleiding voor waterkoeling.
D ❑ verzwakking van de muren rondom het complex.

17 READING

1 Open vragen

Bij deze en de volgende opdracht ga je oefenen met het beantwoorden van *open vragen*. Lees de uitleg over open vragen in *Exam Help* op bladzijde 156 van je *Textbook*.

1 Wat is het belangrijkste verschil tussen het beantwoorden van *citeervragen* en gewone *open vragen?*

Controleer je antwoorden op bladzijde 74 van je *Activity Book*.

2 Examenvraag

Read *Text 17* on page 70 of your Textbook. Answer the exam question.

1 Op grond van welk woord/welke woorden uit de tekst weet je dat je geen geld terugkrijgt als je tijdens een bezoek door omstandigheden met minder mensen zou komen? Citeer (= *schrijf over uit de tekst*) het woord/de woorden uit de tekst. (*1p*)

18 READING

1 Moeilijke woorden

Read *'Turn right' into a porta-potty* on page 71 of your *Textbook*. Look up the following words from the text in your dictionary.

English	Dutch
commands	______________
apparently	______________
error	______________
damage	______________
reckless	______________

Controleer je antwoorden op bladzijde 74 van je *Activity Book*.

2 Exam Question

Read *'Turn right' into a porta-potty* again.

1 'ended up in deep doodoo' (eerste zin) Het artikel gaat over een ongeval. Naar welk deel van het ongeluk verwijst deze uitdrukking? Geef antwoord in het Nederlands. (*1p*)

____

19 READING

1 True/False-vragen

Bij deze en de volgende opdracht ga je oefenen met het beantwoorden van *True/False-vragen*. Lees de uitleg over True/False-vragen in *Exam Help* op bladzijde 156 van je *Textbook*.

De zinnen hieronder gaan over True/False-vragen. Vul de juiste woorden in.

1 Het kan nuttig zijn om ______________ in de bewering te onderstrepen
2 Een bewering is juist als die ______________ betekenis heeft als waarover het tekstgedeelte gaat.
3 Je moet niet te veel kijken naar ______________ in de tekst, maar meer naar het geheel.

Controleer je antwoorden op bladzijde 74 van je *Activity Book*.

2 Examenvraag

Read *The Bramah Museum of Tea and Coffee* on page 71 of your *Textbook.* Answer the exam questions.

Geef van elk van de volgende beweringen aan of deze juist of onjuist is volgens de tekst. (*2p*)

1 Het museum richt zich voornamelijk op de sociale kant van koffie- en theedrinken door de eeuwen heen. *juist / onjuist*
2 Volgens het museum is de smaak van koffie en thee goed, maar het kan misschien nog beter. *juist / onjuist*

3 Alles wat in Londen te maken heeft met thee, vind je vooral op de zuidoever van de Theems. *juist / onjuist*

4 Het drinken van thee 's middags is een nieuwe trend onder de Britse bevolking. *juist / onjuist*

20 READING

1 Gatenteksten

Bij deze en de volgende opdracht ga je oefenen met *gatenteksten.* Lees de uitleg over gatenteksten in *Exam Help* op bladzijde 156 van je *Textbook*.

Maak de zinnen af.

1 Voordat je met de vragen begint, is het goed om ______

2 Om te kunnen achterhalen wat er in het gat past, moet je ______

______

3 Probeer altijd eerst zelf te bedenken ______

4 Onbekende woorden ______

Controleer je antwoorden op bladzijde 74 van je *Activity Book*.

2 Examenvraag

Read *Tuck in ... a quarter of baby food in jars is eaten by adults* on page 73 in your *Textbook*. Answer the questions.

1 Kies bij **–1–** in alinea 1 het juiste antwoord uit de gegeven mogelijkheden. (*1p*)
A ❑ easy to consume
B ❑ good value for money
C ❑ quite tasty
D ❑ rather healthy

2 Kies bij **–2–** in alinea 3 het juiste antwoord uit de gegeven mogelijkheden. (*1p*)
A ❑ Even though
B ❑ Just as
C ❑ Now that

3 Kies bij **–3–** in alinea 4 het juiste antwoord uit de gegeven mogelijkheden. (*1p*)
A ❑ gain strength
B ❑ lose weight
C ❑ prepare meals
D ❑ save time

4 Kies bij **–4–** in alinea 5 het juiste antwoord uit de gegeven mogelijkheden. (*1p*)
A ❑ change our recipes
B ❑ ignore this group
C ❑ settle for continuity
D ❑ target them

5 Kies bij **–5–** in alinea 6 het juiste antwoord uit de gegeven mogelijkheden. (*1p*)
A ❑ affordable
B ❑ available
C ❑ questionable
D ❑ unavoidable

1 Moeilijke woorden

Read *The Truth about Bears* on page 74 of your *Textbook.* Here are some keywords from the text. Guess their meaning and then check with your dictionary.

! If you have to use a dictionary, look at *Woordenboek gebruiken* on page 124 of your *Textbook*.

	My guess	Dictionary
tranquilizers (par.1)		
trap (par.1)		
gain (par. 2)		
explode (par. 2)		
deliberately (par. 3)		
ferocious (par. 4)		
determined (par. 4)		
disrupts (par. 7)		

Controleer je antwoorden op bladzijde 74 van je *Activity Book*.

2 Examenvraag

Read *The Truth about Bears* again. Answer the exam questions.

1 Which of the following about Rogers is true according to paragraph 1? (*1p*)
A ❑ He became interested in live bears after he had first examined dead ones.
B ❑ He failed to understand bears despite spending time and effort on them.
C ❑ He felt he was better at studying bears in the wild than in a laboratory.
D ❑ He objected against scientifically accepted tests which traumatise bears.

2 'to explode myths about them' (alinea 2) In welke alinea worden deze misverstanden over beren verder uitgewerkt? Noteer het nummer van deze alinea. (*1p*) ____________

3 What is the main purpose of paragraph 3? (*1p*)
A ❑ to explain what mistakes Rogers makes when dealing with bears
B ❑ to give a description of the contact between Rogers and the bears
C ❑ to make clear that the bears Rogers works with are not at all dangerous
D ❑ to show the dangers of making *Bearwalker of the Northwoods*

4 How does paragraph 6 connect to paragraph 5? (*1p*)
A ❑ It highlights what is said in paragraph 5.
B ❑ It supports what is said in paragraph 5.
C ❑ It undermines what is said in paragraph 5.

5 Geef van elk van de volgende beweringen aan of deze wel of niet overeenkomt met de inhoud van alinea 7 en 8. Omcirkel achter elk nummer 'wel' of 'niet'. (2*p*)

1	In de academische wereld is Rogers bekend om zijn wetenschappelijke publicaties.	*wel / niet*
2	Andere wetenschappers vinden dat Rogers het gedrag van beren niet goed kan bestuderen door de manier waarop hij met ze omgaat.	*wel / niet*
3	Collega-wetenschappers snappen niet hoe het Rogers lukt om dicht bij de beren te komen.	*wel / niet*
4	Rogers gaat met June om alsof ze een van zijn huisdieren is.	*wel / niet*

22 READING

1 Moeilijke woorden

Read *Yellow Pages* on page 124 of your *Textbook* about how to use your dictionary.

Then read *When Posh met Poor* on page 75 in your *Textbook.* Match the English words from the text with the Dutch meaning. Draw lines.

well-off (par. 1)	uitkering
slang (par. 2)	zwerver
cosy (par. 2)	liefhebbend
bright (par. 3)	dialect
affectionate (par. 4)	slim
benefit (par. 5)	gezellig
resentful (par. 5)	boos
tramp (par 6)	rijk

Controleer je antwoorden op bladzijde 74 van je *Activity Book*.

2 Examenvraag

Read *When Posh met Poor* again. Answer the questions.

1 Kies bij **–1–** in alinea 1 het juiste antwoord uit de gegeven mogelijkheden. (*1p*)
A ❑ quite realistic
B ❑ rather balanced
C ❑ really complicated
D ❑ very one-sided

2 Kies bij **–2–** in alinea 2 het juiste antwoord uit de gegeven mogelijkheden. (*1p*)
A ❑ However
B ❑ Likewise
C ❑ Moreover
D ❑ Therefore

3 Kies bij **–3–** in alinea 2 het juiste antwoord uit de gegeven mogelijkheden. (*1p*)
A ❑ independent
B ❑ romantic
C ❑ traditional

4 '…I know she'll make something of herself,' (alinea 3)
In welke alinea zegt Natalie zelf iets over haar toekomst? (*1p*)
A ❑ alinea 4
B ❑ alinea 5
C ❑ alinea 6
D ❑ alinea 7

5 What becomes clear about Natalie in paragraphs 4 and 5? (*1p*)
A ❑ She dislikes having to spend a lot of time with her brother.
B ❑ She feels it is her responsibility to look after her family.
C ❑ She hated having to go to school when she was younger.

6 Geef voor elk van de volgende beweringen aan of ze wel of niet als overeenkomst tussen Alice en Natalie in de tekst genoemd worden. Omcirkel achter elk zin 'wel' of 'niet'. (*2p*)

1 Ze gebruiken dezelfde straattaal. *wel / niet*

2 Ze zijn bevriend met dezelfde mensen. *wel / niet*

3 Ze vinden dezelfde kleren leuk. *wel / niet*

4 Ze hebben een vergelijkbare band met hun moeder. *wel / niet*

23 WRITING

1 SE-voorbereidingsopdracht

Read *Volunteer opportunities* on page 77 in your *Textbook*. Then write an application letter. Use the points below.

! Look at *Yellow Pages* on page 127 in your*Textbook* about *Het schrijven van een brief of e-mail.*

- Vertel waar je de advertentie hebt gezien.
- Vertel een aantal dingen over jezelf (naam, leeftijd, school, hobby's, enzovoort).
- Schrijf dat je graag als vrijwilliger bij *Safehaven* zou willen werken.
- Noem twee redenen waarom je dat leuk lijkt en vertel wat voor werk je zou willen doen.
- Vertel dat je ook wel een idee hebt om geld in te zamelen: het organiseren van een sponsorloop. Zeg dat je daar al wel wat ervaring mee hebt.
- Bedenk een aantal vragen over het werk als vrijwilliger bij *Safehaven.*
- Sluit de brief op een passende manier af.

24 SPEAKING

1 SE-voorbereidingsopdracht

Read *My daily* routines on page 77 in your *Textbook.* Work together with a classmate. You are going to have a conversation about daily routines. Decide who is pupil A and who is pupil B.

Pupil A Speech card 30
Pupil B Speech card 27

Look up your speech card at the back of your *Activity Book.*

Uitwerkingen

13 Listening

1 1 geweldig; beautiful, good
2 people, special, difficulty, occupation/job
3 B

2 1 B
2 B
3 B
4 A
5 B
6 A
7 C
8 B

3 1 adopted, salad, used, experiments, nature, free, temperature
2 A
3 A

4 1 B
2 B
3 C
4 C
5 A
6 B

14 Watching

1 1 **Paralymics Skiing Fact file**

Onderdeel van	de paralympische winterspelen
Twee paralympic ski-onderdelen	cross country skiën, biathlon
Afstanden	2, 5 km en 20 km
Twee soorten beperkingen	visuele handicaps – lichamelijke handicaps

2 ☐ de enorme kosten die de *Paralympics* met zich meebrengen.
☒ de oprichting en het ontstaan van de *Paralympics*.
☒ de technische hulpmiddelen die beschikbaar zijn voor paralympische sporters.
☐ hoe moeilijk het is om als gehandicapte aan intensieve sport te doen.
☐ tegenstanders van het organiseren van *The Paralympics*.

3 A

2 1 B
2 C
3 C
4 B
5 C
6 A
7 C
8 B

15 Reading

1 ☒ Het is belangrijk om eerst te achterhalen wat voor een tekst je gaat lezen.
☐ Het is nuttig om van tevoren de vraag en de bijbehorende antwoorden te lezen.
☒ Probeer altijd eerst zelf een antwoord te formuleren op de gestelde vraag.
☐ *Skimmen* is hetzelfde als iets heel nauwkeurig lezen.
☒ Voor het beantwoorden van vragen bij korte(re) teksten moet je vaak zoekend lezen.

2 **Examenvraag (2p)**

1 Goed antwoord: C (*He is worried too many children no longer experience controlled risk which would teach them to make safe decisions in the future)*
Fout antwoord A: Ze willen juist voorkomen dat kinderen veel in aanraking komen met (gewelddadige) computerspellen.
Fout antwoord B: De speeltuinen zijn wel uitdagend (*physically challenging)*, maar niet gevaarlijk.
Fout antwoord D: Kinderen moeten er wel leren, maar het zijn geen informative-centra.

2 Goed antwoord: D (...*more catch-up classes and one-to-one tuition with the aim of helping struggling pupils and stimulating the gifted.*)
Fout antwoord A: Hij noemt werkplaatsen, maar dat slaat op de scholen zelf.
Fout antwoord B: Hij heeft het over kinderen die van school gestuurd zijn, niet over thuissituaties.
Fout antwoord C: Hij noemt alleen kinderen die van school zijn gestuurd.

16 Reading

1

Words	**Meaning**
shut down	uitschakelen
clog	verstoppen
clear	schoonmaken
flood	onder water zetten
gob	spuug
bodies	oppervlaktes

2 **Examenvraag (1p)**
Goed antwoord: C (*tonnes of jellyfish clogged the pipes*)
Fout antwoord A: Er was sprake van verstopping, niet van het vastlopen van iets.
Fout antwoord B: Er was geen lekkage.
Fout antwoord D: Muren worden genoemd in verband met een tsunami in Japan.

17 Reading

1 Citeervragen beantwoord je in het Engels (je citeert iets uit de tekst), open vragen in het Nederlands.

2 **Examenvraag (1p)**
(bookings are) non-refundable (er wordt geen geld teruggegeven).

18 Reading

1

English	**Dutch**
commands	aanwijzingen
apparently	blijkbaar
error	fout
damage	schade
reckless	roekeloos/gevaarlijk

2 **Examenvraag (1p)**
De botsing met het toilet.

19 Reading

1 1 Het kan nuttig zijn om **belangrijke delen** in de bewering te onderstrepen.
  2 Een bewering is juist als die **dezelfde** betekenis heeft als waarover het tekstgedeelte gaat.
  3 Je moet niet te veel kijken naar **losse woorden** in de tekst, maar meer naar het geheel.

2 **Examenvraag (2p)**
  1 Onjuist (het vertelt ook de *commercial side*)
  2 Juist (*The museum believes everything possible should be done to maintain and, if possible, improve the quality of tea and coffee...)*
  3 Onjuist (*...on both sides of the Thames*)
  4 Onjuist (geen nieuwe trend: het wordt wel populairder gemaakt)

20 Reading

1 1 Voordat je met de vragen begint, is het goed om *je te oriënteren op de tekst / te kijken wat voor een tekst het is.*
  2 Om te kunnen achterhalen wat er in het gat past, moet je *vaak terug lezen en vooruit lezen.*
  3 Probeer altijd eerst zelf te bedenken *welk (Nederlands) woord er in het gat past.*
  4 Onbekende woorden *moet je opzoeken in het woordenboek.*

2 **Examenvraag (5p)**
  1 A: easy to consume – Volwassenen vinden de babyvoeding zelf ook gemakkelijk en lekker.
  2 A: Even though – In de zin erna wordt een tegenstelling gegeven.
  3 B: lose weight – Vrouwen denken met de voeding te kunnen afvallen.
  4 D: target them – Ze willen volwassenen niet als doel gebruiken om hun product beter te kunnen verkopen. Ze willen vasthouden aan hun 'baby-imago'.
  5 D: unavoidable – Ze raden de voeding alleen aan als het niet anders kan.

21 Reading

1

My guess	**Dictionary**
tranquilizers (par.1)	verdovingsmiddelen
trap (par.1)	val
gain (par. 2)	winnen/behalen
explode (par. 2)	tenietdoen
deliberately (par. 3)	opzettelijk
ferocious (par. 4)	gewelddadig
determined (par. 4)	vastbesloten
disrupts (par. 7)	verstoren

2 **Examenvraag (6p)**
  1 Goed antwoord: B (*None of that allowed him to really know the creatures.*)
  Fout antwoord A: Hij had ze alleen geschoten om ze te verdoven.
  Fout antwoord C: Daarover wordt niets gezegd.
  Fout antwoord D: De beren zouden zijn getraumatiseerd als ze in vallen terecht waren gekomen.

2 Alinea 4 (*...they do not like honey and they are not ferocious.)*

3 Goed antwoord: B (Hij legt uit hoe hij contact maakt met de beren.)
Fout antwoord A: Niet alles gaat altijd goed, maar van fouten wordt niet gesproken.
Fout antwoord C: Dat wordt niet beweerd, wel dat ze vaak nerveus gedrag kunnen vertonen.
Fout antwoord D: Rogers wordt niet nerveus van het gedrag van de beren tijdens het filmen.

4 Goed antwoord: B (Hij bevestigt dat beren niet echt gevaarlijk voor mensen zijn.)
Fout antwoord A: Hij zegt meer dat het gevaar juist van mensen komt.
Fout antwoord C: Hij ondermijnt het niet, hij bevestigt het juist.

5 1 niet: *He does not have a significant publishing record...*
2 wel: *...feeding the animals runs the risk of changing the behaviour you want to study.*
3 niet: *...it's not an approach we use.* Maar dat zegt niets over dichter bij beren komen.
4 niet: *...she doesn't think of me in those terms* (in termen van het houden van huisdieren/honden).

22 Reading

1

well-off (par. 1)	rijk
slang (par. 2)	dialect
cosy (par. 2)	gezellig
bright (par. 3)	slim
affectionate (par. 4)	liefhebbend
benefit (par. 5)	uitkering
resentful (par. 5)	boos
tramp (par. 6)	zwerver

2 Examenvraag (7p)

1 Goed antwoord: D (*I was living in a bubble and believed money made you better than other people*.)

2 Goed antwoord: A (In de regels erna staat een duidelijke tegenstelling met het voorafgaande.)

3 Goed antwoord: A (*She hates being tied down.* Ze is erg onafhankelijk, ze wil dus graag de touwtjes zelf in handen hebben.)

4 Goed antwoord: C (*I've gone back to college. I've always been very ambitious.)*
Fout antwoord A: Daarin wordt meer beschreven hoe ze woont, enzovoort.
Fout antwoord B: Hier gaat het vooral om haar financiële situatie.
Fout antwoord D: Ook hierin wordt niets over haar toekomst gezegd.

5 Goed antwoord: B (*It shouldn't be my task to get Gaby to school, but there's no one else to do it.*)
Fout antwoord A: Ze voelt zich juist verantwoordelijk voor hem.
Fout antwoord C: Ze kon vaak niet naar school vanwege haar thuissituatie.

6 1 wel (*I spoke the same slang as her.*)
2 niet: Dit wordt niet genoemd.
3 wel: (*I really liked the skirt Alice was wearing.*)
4 niet: Er wordt alleen gezegd dat Nathalie een goede verstandhouding heeft met haar moeder.

Resultaat examenvragen

Hieronder kun je zien hoe je ongeveer gescoord zou hebben op het echte examen.
Voor elke examenvraag staat het aantal punten dat je ermee kunt behalen. Dat geldt alleen voor de vragen bij het onderdeel *Reading*.

Tel de punten van de vragen die je goed hebt beantwoord bij elkaar op.

Bij een *open vraag* kun je soms 2 punten scoren als je twee dingen moest opschrijven. Heb je er daarvan één goed, dan heb je 1 punt behaald.

Voor de *juist/onjuist*-vragen geldt het volgende:
4 goed is 2 punten
3 goed is 1 punt
2 of minder goed is 0 punten

Totaalscore:
0-14 = onvoldoende score
15-20 punten = voldoende score
21-25 punten = goede score

Je moet gemiddeld ongeveer 60% van de vragen goed hebben om een voldoende te scoren.

TABLE OF CONTENTS

Reading Matters

2
POEM

A Answer the questions

Read *I Often Contradict Myself* on page 114 of your *Textbook*. Answer the questions.

1 What do you think the word *contradict* means?

2 Look up the word in a dictionary. Did you give the same explanation as the dictionary?

B Answer the questions

Read *I Often Contradict Myself* again and answer the questions.

1 What people do you think often contradict themselves? Why do you think that?

2 Have look at the poem below. Draw lines between the contradictions in the poem.

I often contradict myself.
Oh no, I never do.
I argue with myself day and night.
That simply isn't true.

Oh yes it is. Oh no it's not.
I do this all day long.
Oh no I don't. Oh yes I do.
That's right. No way! It's wrong.

I'm really quite agreeable.
I argue night and day.
I love to be around myself.
I wish I'd go away.

So if you see me arguing,
it's certain that you won't.
I like to contradict myself.
I promise you I don't.

3 Rewrite the first stanza so it does not have any contradictions.

4 Think of five contradictions yourself and write them down.

2

POEM

Ⓒ Do the assignment

Have a look at the list of assignments on page 85. Choose an assignment from category **B**.

Title assignment: ______

4

SHORT STORY

Ⓐ Answer the questions

Read the first paragraph of *The case of the lower case letter* on page 117 of your *Textbook.* Answer the questions.

1 Who is Professor Edgar Nettleston?

2 What is missing? Why does Edith Nettleston want to find it? Explain your answer.

4

SHORT STORY

B Answer the questions

Read *The case of the lower case letter* and answer the following questions.

1 Who is the narrator of this story?

2 '*Mr. Nettleston was a world-renowned lexical semanticist, not a teenager texting his BFFs.*'

Why does the narrator point this out?

3 The narrator also points out that the letter has a more than the usual number of homophones.

What are homophones?

4 Write down the eight homophones from the text and the Dutch translation below.

EN	NL	EN	NL

Now write down the hidden message in Dutch:

5 Read the last paragraph again. Explain how the narrator knows that Edith killed her husbanc.

6 Where exactly does the narrator find the important paper?

C Do the assignment

Have a look at the list of assignments on page 85. Choose an assignment from category **D**.

Title assignment:

4 SHORT STORY

6 NOVEL

A Answer the questions

Have a look at the title and the picture of the book *The Adoration of Jenna Fox* on page 121 of your *Textbook* and answer the questions.

1 What do you think the title means?

2 Who is Jenna Fox, do you think? Explain your answer.

B Answer the questions

Read *The Adoration of Jenna Fox.* Answer the questions.

		true	false
1	Jenna feels comfortable being around her mother.	❑	❑
2	Jenna finds it hard to call her grandmother Nana.	❑	❑
3	It's the first time since her accident that a woman has been elected president.	❑	❑
4	Jenna's accident happened two years ago.	❑	❑
5	Five days after her waking up Jenna could walk without falling.	❑	❑
6	Jenna and her family live in Boston.	❑	❑
7	Jenna cuts herself with a knife.	❑	❑

8 Read the last paragraph again. Why is Jenna upset?

9 What kind of **genre** do you think this novel belongs to? Explain your answer.

6

NOVEL

C Do the assignment

Have a look at the list of assignments on page 85. Choose an assignment from category **A**.

Title assignment: ______________________________

The assignments

Category A: writing about a text

- ❏ **Newspaper article**
  Write a short article for a newspaper covering the events of the text you have just read. Write about 180-200 words. Also think of a good title for your article.

- ❏ **Blurb**
  A *blurb* is the text on the back cover of a book. Generally a *blurb* is made up of a short summary of the book and/or a biography of the author. Short reviews by readers are also often included in the *blurb.* Write a *blurb* for the story that you have just read. Make sure you include what the text is about and why people should read it. Write a blurb of 100-120 words.

- ❏ **Review**
  Give your opinion of the story that you have just read. Explain in 180-200 words why you feel this way. Think of a good title for your review.

- ❏ **Summary**
  Summarise the text that you have just read in a maximum of 120 words. Be careful not to give away the ending.

- ❏ **Songtext**
  Find a songtext that you think fits with the story. Quote (= *citeer*) parts of the songtext that you think portrays the content or the mood of the story. Explain why it fits with the story in 100-120 words.

Category B: (re)writing a text

- ❏ **Prologue to the story**
  What happened before the story began? Describe in 140-160 words one or more events which led up to the beginning of the story.

- ❏ **Plot twists**
  Give the story a new twist halfway through. Write a new middle section of 140-160 words. Describe an event that influences the course of this story.

- ❏ **Different ending**
  Could the story have a different ending? Write a new ending in 140-160 words.

- ❏ **Follow-up of the story**
  What happens after the ending of the story? Write a follow-up of the story in 140-160 words.

Category C: writing to, about or from the point of view of a character

❑ **Interview**
Which of the characters in the story would you like to interview if you were a journalist? Write an interview in which you ask one of the main characters 4-6 questions. Think of answers that would be in line with the contents of the story. Use 120-140 words.

❑ **Message**
Write a message of 120-140 words to one of the characters in the story in which you, for example, warn, advise, or reprimand them.

❑ **Diary fragment**
Write a section of the diary of the most important person in the story (according to you). Use 120-140 words.

❑ **Another lead character**
Write a part of the story from the perspective of a different character. Choose one of the other characters in the story to be the main character. Describe an event from his or her perspective in 120-140 words.

Category D: depicting a text (individually or in pairs)

❑ **Drawing or collage**
Illustrate the events in the story with your own drawings or with existing images (for example from magazines or newspapers).

❑ **Comic**
Turn (part of) the text into a comic story. Draw the main storyline of the text or one of the scenes in at least four comic frames.

❑ **Book cover**
Design a book cover to go with the text that you have read. Design the back and front cover of the book. Make sure that the cover of the book matches the contents as well as the tone of the book.

❑ **Film scene**
Work together with one or more classmates. Choose a fragment from the text and act it out. The scene may last up to 3 minutes. Use a camera or a phone to record the result.

TABLE OF CONTENTS

Bridging the Gap
mbo
Brug van klas 4 naar mbo

1 Administrative and clerical services

A

WORDS

1 Solve the puzzle

Study *Words* on page 173 of your *Textbook*. Write down the English translations of the Dutch words below. Then find the English words in the word search. Make sure you look in all directions. Before you do this exercise, study *Woordenboek gebruiken* on page 124 of your *Textbook*.

balans ______________________

bedrijfstak ______________________

belasting ______________________

bevestigen ______________________

boekhouden ______________________

btw ______________________

dossierkast ______________________

efficiënt ______________________

onderhandelingen ______________________

ontvangsthal ______________________

overgeplaatst ______________________

proefperiode ______________________

schema ______________________

startersfunctie ______________________

toegangspasje ______________________

uitstellen ______________________

N	R	Z	B	B	X	W	E	B	S	Z	V	E	U	E	F
E	A	A	P	A	M	E	N	O	R	N	R	A	Z	Z	F
G	E	A	U	L	S	Z	T	O	E	L	A	Y	T	F	I
O	F	M	G	A	K	L	R	K	C	G	S	E	B	D	L
T	F	Z	M	N	A	T	Y	K	E	X	C	G	H	I	I
I	I	T	Q	C	T	R	-	E	P	P	H	G	T	N	N
A	C	R	U	E	I	I	L	E	T	O	E	E	Q	D	G
T	I	A	A		Z	A	E	P	I	S	D	N	W	U	
I	E	N	U	S	A	L	V	I	O	T	U	T	Q	S	C
O	N	S	P	H	A		E	N	N	P	L	R	H	T	A
N	T	F	D	E	M	P	L	G		O	E	Y	G	R	B
S	T	E	E	E	L	E		C	H	N	A	P	W	Y	I
G	D	R	P	T	H	R	J	O	A	E	A	A	I	R	N
U	D	R	T	A	T	I	O	N	L	G	B	S	L	X	E
U	A	E	F	A	L	O	B	H	L	G	M	S	D	S	T
P	Y	D	T	A	X	D	C	O	N	F	I	R	M	L	X

2 Complete the forum

Have another look at *Words*. Complete the forum posts below.

access – be in charge of – brief – executive – inconvenient – policy – storage – temp

Back Forward Stop Refresh Home Search Favorites History Mail Print

www.forum.co.uk

Agenda | Restaurants | Drinks | Magazines | **Forum**

Office supplies costs

We're having a real problem with keeping office supply costs in check. The number of pens, pencils and sticky notes we go through is staggering and expensive. We have posted signs reminding people that these costs add up. It doesn't seem to have much effect, however. Any tips are welcome.

Lauryn

Posted at 11:17

We keep everything in a locked **(1)** ____________________ Only the administration and myself as manager have **(2)** ____________________ to the room. Also, when we have a new **(3)** ____________________, we set up their desk with essentials only. It is a cost-saving method that works really well.

Simon

Posted at 13:38

If posting notes is not sufficient you should **(4)** ____________________ your colleagues about it. Or maybe your **(5)** ____________________ should discuss the issue during a staff meeting. Most likely your colleagues will listen to the boss. ;-) I can tell from experience that this is the only way! In my former job I used to **(6)** ____________________ office supplies.

Denise

Posted at 15:49

Most of our supplies are locked away. We have also recently started using 'shared' items, like Tipp-ex, that must be returned when the user is done. No one is happy about the new rules. It can be a bit **(7)** ____________________ at times because you're always looking for things! However, this new **(8)** ____________________ does seem to work because we've managed to keep things in stock longer that way.

Adapted from: businessmanagementdaily.com

B

DIALOGUE

3 Complete the dialogue

Study *Introductions* on page 173 of your *Textbook*. Complete the dialogue below. Use the clues in brackets and phrases from the *Introductions*.

Danny: Excuse me, is this Mr Nilson's office?

Mr Nilson: Come in. You must be our new intern. **(1)** ______________________________ *(aangenaam kennismaken)*

Welcome to Greenway's. **(2)** ______________________________

(naam – Edmund Nilson – en – verantwoordelijk voor – boekhouden)

It's also part of my job to guide new interns so they get used to the company.

Danny: Hello Mr Nilson. I'm Danny Simpson. **(3)** ______________________________ *(kijk ernaar uit – hier te werken – als stagiair)*

Mr Nilson: I'm sure you will! If I'm correct, you're going to work in the mail room. You'll help deliver letters and packages to all floors.

Danny: Yes, as I understand it, that will be one of my duties here.

Mr Nilson: **(4)** ______________________________ *(leuk vinden – ontmoeten – je nieuwe collega's?)*

Danny: **(5)** ______________________________ *(leuk – leren kennen)*

Mr Nilson: All right. Please follow me then. I'll give you a short tour.

First **(6)** ______________________________

(ga je ontmoeten – mijn secretaresse – op de tweede verdieping werkt)

She will provide you with some general information that will come in handy when you work here.

Danny: Sounds like a plan!

4 Write the email

You're the new intern at a company. Write a short email to the team you will be working with. You can make up what sort of company you're interning for.

Tip Before you do this exercise, read *Het schrijven van een brief of e-mail* in the *Yellow Pages* on page 127 of your *Textbook*.

Make sure you:
- explain who you are
- give information about yourself (for example your education)
- explain in which room / where in the building you work (you can make this up)
- invite them to get in contact with you personally, if they wish

Use *Introductions* and write 100-120 words.

Send Quote Address Attach Options Spelling Save Security Stop

To:

Subject:

Kind regards,

C
READING

5 Answer the questions

Read *Whoa! An administrative assistant does* ALL *that?* on page 174 of your *Textbook*. Answer the questions.

1 What is said about the role of an administrative assistant in the company according to the first paragraph?

2 Who are the people administrative assistants usually work with?

3 Mention five common tasks for administrative assistants.

4 Write down in your own words the most important downsides and benefits of being an administrative assistant.

–

\+

5 Would you like to be an administrative assistant? Why (not)? Use information from the text to support your answer.

2 Welfare

A

WORDS

1 Fill in the grid

Study *Words* on page 175 of your *Textbook*. Write the words in the correct columns and write down the Dutch translation. Use a dictionary if necessary.

appointment – bandage – consultation hours – dentistry – GP – social workers – surgeon – treatment – walker – wheelchair

Medical equipment and products	**Dutch**
Medical areas and professions	
Seeing the doctor	

2 Circle the correct alternative

Have a look at *Words* again. Circle the correct alternatives in the sentences below.

1 GP practices, dental practices and hospitals all provide *health care / home care*.

2 The term mental *disorder / disability* is commonly used for mental illnesses.

3 Can you hand me a *nappy / filling*? The baby needs a change.

4 The doctor gave me a *prescription / social security number* for the medication.

5 Your *pulse / upbringing* influences the way you behave when you have grown up.

6 You first have to find a vein before you can *administer a drip / treat*.

7 Maurice's injuries aren't severe. The doctors think he will *recover / tackle* soon.

B

DIALOGUE

3 Say it in English

Study *The internship* on page 175 of your *Textbook*. Write down the correct English translations of the sentences below.

1 Een van mijn taken is om wonden te behandelen.

2 Je moet vragen stellen aan de maatschappelijk werkers.

3 We moeten observeren hoe huisartsen met hun patiënten communiceren.

4 Mijn docent instrueerde me om te letten op de behandelingen die de verpleegkundigen verrichten.

5 Na een maand zal ik met verpleegkundigen meelopen om het werk te leren.

6 Ik zal eerst leren hoe ik verbanden moet aanbrengen.

4 Write the email

You're an intern at a company in the healthcare sector (for example a dental practice, home care, a child day care centre). You send an email to a friend about your internship.

! **Tip** Before you do this exercise, read *Het schrijven van een brief of e-mail* in the *Yellow Pages* on page 127 of your *Textbook*.

Make sure you:
- give details about what kind of internship you do and where
- mention four different tasks you perform during the internship
- mention a task that you like or dislike

Use *The internship* and write 100-120 words.

Send Quote Address Attach Options Spelling Save Security Stop

To:

Subject:

5 Correct the mistakes

Read *Working as a dental nurse* on page 176 of your *Textbook*. The sentences below are about the text but each one contains a mistake. Cross out the mistake and write the correct information below the sentence.

1 Een belangrijk onderdeel van Sophies werk is patiënten geruststellen in de wachtkamer.

2 De tandartspraktijk waar Sophie werkt, doet alleen standaardbehandelingen.

3 Sophie maakt alles schoon aan het begin van de werkdag.

4 Sophie haalt de meeste voldoening uit het werken met de modernste tandartsapparatuur.

5 Het doel van de tandartspraktijk is om zo veel mogelijk patiënten aan te trekken.

6 Sophie adviseerde een filmster om naar Braden Dental Care te gaan voor een gratis controle.

3 Engineering and construction

A
WORDS

1 Fill in the words

Study *Words* on page 177 of your *Textbook*. Write down the words for the numbered items in the image. There are two words you can't use. Use a dictionary if necessary. Choose from:

arch – building plan – calculations – construction site – license – mason – safety measures – sewer system – to weld – wiring

1 ______________________
2 ______________________
3 ______________________
4 ______________________
5 ______________________
6 ______________________
7 ______________________
8 ______________________

2 Write down the words

Have another look at *Words*. The letters of the words below have been mixed up. Put the letters in the correct order and write down the correct English words. Then write down the Dutch translations. The first letter of each word is printed **bold**. Use a dictionary if necessary.

		English	Dutch
1	erbdherusifb	refurbished	opgeknapt
2	eresxipet		
3	yerda ofr seu		
4	orwdkoow		

5 slecine

6 aenhmcailc egeernin

7 ot ets

8 ayretcnpr

9 aelrnuotgsi

10 iteandr sa

11 idergeetrs

12 ocrnolt alpen

13 owopkhrs

14 ot ncncoet

15 lacociultans

16 lurepbm

B

DIALOGUE

3 Put in the correct order

Study *Cutting edge* on page 177 of your *Textbook*. Make sentences by putting the words in the correct order. Next, write down the Dutch translation.

1 start – you – the emergency stop – off – up – by switching – the machine

EN

NL

2 into – the control panel – you – plug – the cable – first

EN

NL

3 check – if – connected – the fridge – is – you – electricity – should – to

EN

NL

4 you have – after – on – the wiring – switch – you can – it – checked

EN

NL

5 how – is – the last step – connect – the air pump – you – to the filter

EN

NL

6 else – to twist – you – the button – nothing – have – or – happens

EN

NL

4 Write the instructions

Have another look at *Cutting edge*. Your teacher asks you to write user instructions for a machine. Below you can see a picture of a *floor tile cutter* (tegelzaagmachine). You can write instructions for this machine but you can also choose another machine that is used in engineering or construction.

Tip Before you do this exercise, read *Tips bij het schrijven* in the *Yellow Pages* on page 127 of your *Textbook*.

Make sure you:
- explain in at least four steps how to use the machine (you can make these up)
- write short, clear sentences
- mention some safety instructions for using the machine

Use *Cutting edge* and write 100-120 words. Use a dictionary if necessary.

5 Choose the correct answer

Read *How do I become… a superyacht builder?* on page 178 of your *Textbook*. Tick the correct answers.

1 What becomes clear about Niels van Dinther?
A ❑ He got hired as a superyacht builder after a four-year apprenticeship.
B ❑ He oversees the building of superyachts and looks after apprentices.

2 In what way have superyachts changed over the years?
A ❑ Their popularity has grown a lot in recent years.
B ❑ They have become smaller but more expensive.

3 What does Van Dinther say about the yachts they produce?
A ❑ A lot of yachts have to be adjusted during construction because of the owners' wishes.
B ❑ Because of technological developments the yachts can be constructed faster than before.

4 What is a trend in modern superyachts?
A ❑ a focus on decoration and gadgets
B ❑ a return to tradition and craft

5 Do you need boat experience to get selected for an apprenticeship at Pendennis Shipyard?
A ❑ No, you can also get in if you show you can learn new skills easily.
B ❑ Yes, only people with sailing or boating experience are chosen.

4 Commerce

A
WORDS

1 Find the odd one out

Study *Words* on page 179 of your *Textbook*. In each of the following groups of words, one word does not belong. Write down which word is the odd one out and explain in Dutch why you think so. Use a dictionary if necessary.

1 stock – responsibility – availability – catalogue ____________

____

2 shop window – detection gates – fitting room – launch ____________

____

3 terms of delivery – to gain some experience – to deliver – warehouse ____________

____

4 shift – manufacturer – merchandise – trade fair ____________

____

2 Solve the puzzle

Have another look at *Words*. Translate the words below into English and write the translations in the puzzle.

Down

1 winstgevend
2 klantgericht
3 garantie
4 de deal sluiten
5 kleine zelfstandige

Across

6 verkoopafdeling
7 rondkijken (in een winkel)
8 afleverpunt

3 Make the correct combinations

Study *New desk lamps* on page 179 of your *Textbook*. Make correct sentences by using one phrase from each column in the grid below. Then write down the Dutch translations.

Our company	your new catalogue	sell these products.
Unfortunately	send the merchandise	for car parts with you before.
We would need	has placed orders	by next week.
Is there	add this item	I can do for you?
Could you	we no longer	to our main office?
We are going to	anything else	to our new summer collection.

1 EN ______

NL ______

2 EN ______

NL ______

3 EN ______

NL ______

4 EN ______

NL ______

5 EN ______

NL ______

6 EN ______

NL ______

4 Write the email

You want to order supplies from a catalogue. First decide which products (and how many) you want to order. Then write a short email to the distributor.

! **Tip** Before you do this exercise, read *Het schrijven van een brief of e-mail* in the *Yellow Pages* on page 127 of your *Textbook*.

Make sure you:
- introduce yourself and the company you work for
- mention which products you've already purchased from the distributor
- mention the products from their catalogue you intend to buy
- ask for more information about these products, for example availability or colour
- ask about discounts because of the amount you plan to order
- ask about the details of the delivery, for example when or how
- finish your email in an appropriate way

Use *New desk lamps* and write 100-120 words.

Send Quote Address Attach Options Spelling Save Security Stop

To:

Subject:

C

READING

5 Answer the questions

Read *A day in the life of a shopkeeper* on page 180 of your *Textbook* and indicate whether the statements are true or false.

		true	false
1	David has fixed working days from Monday to Friday.	❑	❑
2	David has helped design the new kitchen department.	❑	❑
3	Visitors can have breakfast at the showroom until 10 o'clock.	❑	❑
4	David's appointment schedule fills up quickly.	❑	❑
5	Ikea employees can have lunch at different restaurants.	❑	❑
6	David usually comes home late because a lot of things have to be finished at the end of the day.	❑	❑

5 Green

A
WORDS

1 Write down the words

Look at *Words* on page 181 of your *Textbook*. Read the description of the words. Then write the correct word behind each description. Use a dictionary if necessary.

	English word
1 a system of keeping animals in indoor farms, often with little space for the animals	....
2 a group of animals or plants that share certain characteristics	....
3 a large container into which people throw away glass objects	....
4 to make a hole in the ground	....
5 environmentally friendly	....
6 a bunch of flowers, cut and tied together	....
7 cows and bulls	....
8 the type of environment that an animal usually lives in	....
9 an area of land that is protected to keep the animals and plants that live there safe	....
10 to keep animals to produce more animals	....
11 a small curled up part of a plant that will open to form a leaf or flower	....
12 to plant seeds in the ground	....
13 an official document which says that you are allowed to do something	....
14 the central part of a plant on which the flowers and leaves grow	....

A

WORDS

2 Complete the text

Have a look at *Words* again. Complete the text below by filling in the correct words. Choose from:

agriculture – combat pests – crop – greenhouse – maintain – nutrition – orchard – organic – supervise – weed

Farming Forward

In this week's *Green Industries* we focus on the future of

(1) ______________________ We kick off with an interview with Robert McSweeney, a Welsh farmer who has won prestigious awards for his innovative ways of farming.

Could you tell us a bit about yourself? You're an (2) ______________________ **farmer. What does that mean?**

For one thing it means I don't use chemicals to grow my vegetables. Also, we use different ways to remove the **(3)** ______________________ from our fields. Instead of using herbicides we do it by hand-picking.

And how do you (4) ______________________ **and diseases?**

There are plenty of methods to tackle these problems. You can place natural predators of the pests onto the crops or you simply pick pests such as caterpillars off the plants by hand. Right now we produce all our food outdoors, but we have plans to build a huge **(5)** ______________________ in which we will grow tomatoes. The best part of growing vegetables indoors is that you don't have to worry about pests and weather conditions.

What are your responsibilities?

My main job is to **(6)** ______________________ the farm workers who perform day-to-day duties, such as planting and harvesting crops. As I mentioned earlier, it takes a lot of time to **(7)** ______________________ the vegetable gardens.

How is this year's harvest?

This year we've produced a fine **(8)** ______________________ of fruit. Our **(9)** ______________________ is doing really well. We've got pears the size of softballs. You should try them. They taste great and, what's more, they provide more **(10)** ______________________ than conventionally grown pears.

Robert, thank you for this interview!

3 Make the correct combinations

Study *Classroom announcement* on page 181 of your *Textbook*. Make correct sentences by drawing lines.

Kieron did most of his work placement	was a wonderful experience.
She has recently completed	he inspected the health and welfare of livestock.
We'd like to invite you	I'd like to take you all out to dinner.
I gained a lot of practical	at a garden centre.
To celebrate the end of my internship	her animal care courses.
While he worked there,	skills in different areas.
After lunch I would	for a tour of the farm.
In short, my work placement	like to take a group picture.

4 Write the invitation

You've just completed your work placement (you can make this up). You send an invitation to your friends and family to celebrate this at a special location.

Tip Before you do this exercise, read *Het schrijven van een brief of e-mail* in the *Yellow Pages* on page 127 of your *Textbook*.

Make sure you:
- mention your reason for writing the email
- mention four tasks you had or special activities you participated in during your apprenticeship
- explain what the apprenticeship has brought you
- include details such as time and location of the celebration

Use *Classroom announcement* and write 100-120 words.

Send Quote Address Attach Options Spelling Save Security Stop

To:

Subject:

C

READING

5 Complete the sentences

Read *Neil Lincoln, fish farmer* on page 182 of your *Textbook*. Complete the sentences by using information from the text.

1 Het werk bij Calverton Fish Farm bestaat voornamelijk uit

2 Neils hobby is

3 Neil hoorde voor het eerst over 'fishfarming' via

4 De twee stages die Neil voor zijn studie heeft gedaan, waren bij

en

5 Neil heeft veel geleerd van

6 Neil heeft de ambitie om

7 Neil hoopt dat hij nooit meer weg hoeft te gaan, omdat

TABLE OF CONTENTS

Bridging the Gap
havo

Brug van 4 vmbo naar 4 havo

Bridging the Gap havo

A
VOCABULARY

1 Solve the puzzle

Look at the *Vocabulary* on page 184 of your *Textbook*. Find the correct *Vocabulary* words for the descriptions and write them in the puzzle.

1 easy to reach or get into
2 the people who control a country
3 suitable
4 situation in which life is very difficult
5 to come to a decision
6 to find a solution
7 detailed and exact
8 low opinion of your own importance
9 extremely good or impressive
10 to make something start
11 very interesting

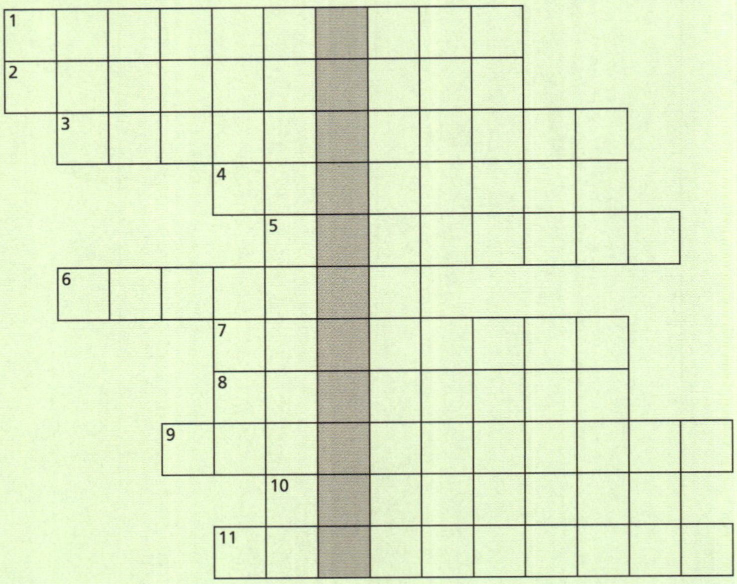

Which word can you read in the grey boxes: ______

In Dutch this word means: ______

2 Fill in the words

Have a look at the words from the *Vocabulary* below. Complete the sentences by filling in the correct words. Use a dictionary if necessary.

acquire – adjust – baffle – defendant – generosity – graduate – lawsuit – negligence – plaintiff – preference – prolific – take charge

1 An example of ______ is when you like tea more than coffee.
2 His ridiculous behaviour never ceases to ______ me.
3 A ______ is someone who has received a degree from a school.
4 Mr Davidson's ______ to those in need is remarkable! He donated half his salary to the poor!
5 ______ means 'to fail to do what should have been done'.

6 According to many Stephen King is a great writer, but he's also a very ______________ writer because he has written dozens of books.

7 In legal cases, the person accused of a crime is called the ______________

8 The person who begins a ______________ is called the ______________

9 She followed the course to ______________ some customer service skills.

10 It can be hard, but people should always ______________ of their own lives. Nobody else can do it for them.

11 Nigella needed some time to ______________ to the idea of moving somewhere else.

B
WATCHING

3 Tick the correct statements

Read the statements below. Then watch *Wannabe writer*. Tick the boxes of the statements that are correct. There are no pauses.

- ❑ Lucy writes from her own experience.
- ❑ At the moment Lucy focuses on writing poems.
- ❑ Lucy believes you can get your inspiration from anything.
- ❑ Lucy says that if you're not sure what to write about, you should take a short break.
- ❑ Most Harold Pinter plays are situated in just one place.
- ❑ Lucy recommends *Pride and Prejudice* because of the language.
- ❑ Lucy gets advice on new books to read through the internet.
- ❑ Lucy's dream job is to become a playwright.

C
READING

4 True or false?

Read *The seven stories* on page 185 of your *Textbook*. Indicate whether the statements are true or false.

		true	false
1	All plots are based on some basic themes.	❑	❑
2	Mrs Post's assignment was simple, because there was only one basic plot in the book.	❑	❑
3	The author saw the film with an open mind, because he had read the book.	❑	❑
4	Katniss thought she wouldn't be able to survive the Games.	❑	❑
5	In The Hunger Games a giant monster attacked the government.	❑	❑
6	Katniss has to go on a journey in order to stay alive.	❑	❑
7	The author of the text didn't expect humour in *The Hunger Games*.	❑	❑
8	After Katniss has lost the final battle she returns to her town.	❑	❑

C

READING

5 Write the sentences

Read *The seven stories* again. Write down in keywords how the seven stories mentioned in the text are present in *The Hunger Games*.

1 Story 1 overcoming the monster: ______________________________

2 Story 2 from rags to riches: ______________________________

3 Story 3 the quest: ______________________________

4 Story 4 going on a voyage: ______________________________

5 Story 5 humor: ______________________________

6 Story 6 tragedy: ______________________________

7 Story 7 rebirth: ______________________________

D

SPEAKING
WRITING

6 Play the role

First read *'Hot Coffee' Redux: NC Jury Tosses Ridiculous Spilled Coffee Lawsuit Against Starbucks* on page 186 of your *Textbook*.

Next work with a classmate. Decide who is pupil A and who is pupil B.

Pupil A speech card 19
Pupil B speech card 25

Look up your speech card in *Talking Matters* at the back of your *Activity Book*.

! **Tip** Before you do this exercise, read *Een gesprek voeren* in the *Yellow Pages* on page 126 of your *Textbook*.

7 Write the letter

Imagine one of the following situations happened to you.

A While working on your laptop in a restaurant you spill your milkshake over your laptop. It wasn't really your mistake as the table was very shaky.

B You tripped over a 'wet floor' sign in a restaurant and hurt your arm. It was dark so you didn't see the sign and the floor was still wet. You can't go to school nor your part-time job at the super market.

C You just bought new inline skates. When you go out inline-skating two of the wheels break off and you skid off the road and hit a tree. You injure your knee and can't go to work or practise any sports for the next four weeks.

D Another situation (you can make this up yourself).

Decide which situation to choose for your letter. Next write a letter to a lawyer about the incident that happened to you.

Tip Before you do this exercise, read *Het schrijven van een brief of e-mail* in the *Yellow Pages* on page 127 of your *Textbook*.

Make sure you:
- explain what and when it happened
- describe what impact it had on you
- clearly express how you would like to resolve the matter (do you want financial compensation or something else in return)
- state in what way you want the lawyer to help you in this matter
- state that you want the lawyer to explain all your possibilities and your chances in court

Write 120-130 words in total.

Dear Madam/Sir,

Yours sincerely,

Speech card 17

Situatie
Je legt je klasgenoot in het kort uit wat voor onderzoek je wilt uitvoeren.

Kies een van de volgende onderzoeksvragen (of verzin zelf een onderzoeksvraag):
A Maakt het eten van chocola je echt gelukkiger?
B Hebben muzikanten een beter geheugen dan andere mensen?
C Beïnvloedt het weer ons humeur?

Verwerk de volgende onderdelen in het gesprek met je klasgenoot:
– wat het onderwerp van je onderzoek is
– hoe je het wilt onderzoeken (bijvoorbeeld door een enquête of door observaties)
– welke uitkomsten je verwacht

Je presentatie moet 1 tot 2 minuten duren. Gebruik *Stone 10.* Beantwoord na afloop vragen van je klasgenoot.

Maak aantekeningen over je onderzoek door in Engelse *keywords* op te schrijven wat je wilt vertellen.

Wissel na het gesprek van rol. Ga naar *Speech card 20*.

Speech card 18

Situatie
Je werkt als reisagent bij een reisbureau. Er komt een klant langs die graag op vakantie wil naar India of Jamaica, maar niet veel van de landen af weet. De klant wil ook graag een feestdag in een van deze landen meemaken. Maak vergelijkingen tussen beide landen. Gebruik hiervoor de informatie uit de tabel.

	India	**Jamaica**
Weer en klimaat	*meestal warm en vochtig – maar kan ook erg nat zijn*	*tropisch – altijd warm*
Beroemd/ bekend van	*Taj Mahal (beroemd gebouw) – grootste filmindustrie*	*Usain Bolt – atletiek – reggae muziek – prachtige natuur*
Bevolking	*erg dichtbevolkt – arm*	*dunbevolkt – grote verschillen in rijkdom*
Nationale feestdag	*Divali – mensen verlichten hun huizen – vuurwerk*	*Independence Day – vroeger kolonie van Groot-Brittanië – muziek, dans, optochten*

– Jij begint het gesprek door de klant te begroeten.
– Beantwoord de vragen van de klant over beide landen.
– Gebruik *Stones 13* en *14*.

Wissel na het gesprek van rol. Ga naar *Speech card 24*.

Speech card 19

Situatie
Tijdens een bezoek aan een koffiezaak mors je een hete koffie over je kleding. Je gaat je beklag doen bij de eigenaar van de zaak.

- Jij begint het gesprek.
- Vertel wat er is gebeurd.
- Leg uit dat de schuld (gedeeltelijk) en verantwoordelijkheid bij de zaak ligt en vertel waarom (bijvoorbeeld omdat de plastic deksel er niet goed op was gedaan, de beker te vol was, de beker erg glad was).
- Vertel wat je van de eigenaar verwacht om het goed te maken en doe hiervoor een voorstel (bijvoorbeeld een jaar lang gratis koffie of 10 keer gratis koffie van de zaak).
- Sluit het gesprek op een gepaste manier af.

Maak voordat je het gesprek begint aantekeningen over wat je wilt zeggen. Gebruik eventueel ook woorden of zinsdelen uit de tekst in je gesprek.

___

___

___

___

___

Wissel na het gesprek van rol. Ga naar *Speech card 29*.

Speech card 20

Situatie
Je klasgenoot vertelt over een onderzoekje dat hij/zij wil uitvoeren. Luister goed naar zijn of haar presentatie en schrijf tijdens het luisteren drie vragen op die je je klasgenoot wilt stellen na afloop.

1 ___

2 ___

3 ___

TALKING MATTERS

Speech card 21

Situatie
Je wilt graag op vakantie, maar je twijfelt tussen India en Jamaica. Je zou ook graag een feestdag willen meemaken in een van beide landen. Je gaat naar het reisbureau om informatie over beide landen te krijgen. Vul de tabel in door vragen te stellen aan de reisagent.

	India	**Jamaica**
Weer en klimaat		
Beroemd/bekend van		
Bevolking		
Nationale feestdag		

- Je klasgenoot begint het gesprek.
- Vraag de reisagent naar informatie over beide landen.
- Gebruik *Stone 13* en *14*.

Wissel na het gesprek van rol. Ga naar *Speech card 28*.

Speech card 22

Situatie
Je klasgenoot vertelt over een onderzoekje dat hij/zij wil uitvoeren. Luister goed naar zijn of haar presentatie en schrijf tijdens het luisteren drie vragen op die je je klasgenoot wilt stellen na afloop.

1 ____________________

2 ____________________

3 ____________________

Wissel na het gesprek van rol. Ga naar *Speech card 26*.

Speech card 23

Situatie
Je bent totaal niet tevreden over het kapsel dat de kapper bij je heeft geknipt. Ondanks jouw duidelijke instructies heeft de kapper zijn werk niet goed gedaan. De kapper vindt dat hem niks te verwijten valt. Je gaat je beklag doen bij de eigenaar van de kapperszaak.

- Jij begint het gesprek.
- Vertel wat er gebeurd is.
- Leg uit welke fouten de kapper heeft gemaakt.
- Vertel wat je van de eigenaar verwacht om het goed te maken en doe hiervoor een voorstel (bijvoorbeeld een jaar lang gratis knipbeurten of geld terug en de volgende keer een gratis knipbeurt).
- Sluit het gesprek op een gepaste manier af.

Maak voordat je het gesprek begint aantekeningen over wat je wilt zeggen.

Speech card 24

Situatie
Je wilt graag op vakantie, maar je twijfelt tussen Zuid-Afrika en Nieuw-Zeeland. Je zou ook graag een feestdag willen meemaken in een van beide landen. Je gaat naar het reisbureau om informatie over beide landen te krijgen. Vul de tabel in door vragen te stellen aan de reisagent.

	Zuid-Afrika	**Nieuw-Zeeland**
Weer en klimaat		
Beroemd/bekend van		
Bevolking		
Nationale feestdag		

- Je klasgenoot begint het gesprek.
- Vraag de reisagent naar informatie over beide landen.
- Gebruik *Stones 13 en 14*.

Speech card 25

Situatie
Je bent de eigenaar van een koffiezaak. Een klant komt klagen omdat hij/zij koffie gemorst heeft en stelt jou daar verantwoordelijk voor.

- Je klasgenoot (de klant) begint het gesprek.
- Luister naar de klant en vraag hoe het met hem/haar gaat na het incident.
- Vertel dat je het erg vervelend vindt dat dit gebeurd is.
- Reageer op wat je klasgenoot voorstelt om de zaak af te handelen.
- Sluit het gesprek op een gepaste manier af.

Maak voordat je het gesprek begint aantekeningen over hoe je wilt reageren en wat je wilt zeggen tegen de klant.

Wissel na het gesprek van rol. Ga naar *Speech card 23*.

Speech card 26

Situatie
Je legt je klasgenoot in het kort uit wat voor onderzoek je wilt uitvoeren.

Kies een van de volgende onderzoeksvragen (of verzin zelf een onderzoeksvraag).
A Is er een verband tussen je kledingstijl en je persoonlijkheid?
B Hebben mannen en vrouwen verschillende favoriete kleuren?
C Hoe reageren mensen op hun omgeving als ze opeens tijdelijk niets kunnen ruiken?

Maak aantekeningen over je onderzoek door in Engelse *keywords* op te schrijven wat je wilt vertellen.

Verwerk de volgende onderdelen in het gesprek met je klasgenoot:
- wat het onderwerp van je onderzoek is
- hoe je het wilt onderzoeken (bijvoorbeeld door een enquête of door observaties)
- welke uitkomsten je verwacht

Je presentatie moet 1 tot 2 minuten duren. Gebruik de *Stone*. Beantwoord na afloop vragen van je klasgenoot.

Speech card 27

Situatie
Je bent een Engels(e) meisje/jongen en je raakt in gesprek met iemand op een camping over hoe een gemiddelde dag/week eruitziet. Gebruik onderstaande gegevens om een goedlopend gesprek te voeren.

- Groet terug en zeg hoe het met je gaat.
- Zeg dat je het ook wel leuk vindt om iets van hem/haar te horen over dagelijkse routines.
- Beantwoord zijn/haar vragen.
- Stel dan hetzelfde soort vragen ook aan hem/haar.
- Reageer op zijn/haar uitnodiging. Bedenk zelf eventueel ook een leuke alternatieve activiteit.
- Sluit het gesprek op een passende manier af.

- Je klasgenoot begint het gesprek.
- Bereid je rol eerst even voor.

Speech card 28

Situatie
Je werkt als reisagent bij een reisbureau. Er komt een klant langs die graag op vakantie wil naar India of Jamaica, maar niet veel van de landen weet. De klant wil ook graag een feestdag in een van deze landen meemaken. Maak vergelijkingen tussen beide landen. Gebruik hiervoor de informatie uit de tabel.

	Zuid-Afrika	**Nieuw-Zeeland**
Weer en klimaat	*verschilt over hele land – aan kust wat koeler – niet tropisch warm*	*vaak warm – westkust meer regen dan oostkust*
Beroemd/bekend van	*Nelson Mandela – prachtige natuurparken – veel wilde dieren*	*prachtige natuur – Maori – kiwivogel*
Bevolking	*50 miljoen – redelijk welvarend*	*rijk – welvarend*
Nationale feestdag	*Heritage Day – Zuid-Afrikanen vieren hun cultuur – dans, theater, goed eten*	*Anzac Day – Nieuw-Zeeland en Australië herdenken slachtoffers in oorlogen – ceremonies en optochten*

- Jij begint het gesprek door de klant te begroeten.
- Beantwoord de vragen van de klant over beide landen.
- Gebruik *Stones 13 en 14*.

Speech card 29

Situatie
Je bent de eigenaar van een kapperszaak. Een klant komt klagen, omdat hij/zij totaal niet tevreden is over zijn/haar nieuwe kapsel.

- Je klasgenoot begint het gesprek.
- Luister naar de klant en vraag wat er precies aan de hand is.
- Vertel dat je het erg vervelend vindt dat dit gebeurd is.
- Reageer op wat je klasgenoot voorstelt om de zaak af te handelen.
- Sluit het gesprek op een gepaste manier af.

Maak voordat je het gesprek begint aantekeningen over hoe je wilt reageren en wat je wilt zeggen tegen de klant.

Speech card 30

Situatie
Je raakt op een camping in Engeland in gesprek met een Engels(e) meisje/jongen over wat jullie dagelijks zoal doen en hoe een gemiddelde week eruitziet. Gebruik onderstaande gegevens om een gesprek daarover te voeren.

- Begroet hem/haar en vraag hoe het met hem/haar gaat.
- Zeg dat je wel graag iets zou weten over zijn/haar dagelijkse bezigheden.
- Vraag hoe een gemiddelde schooldag van hem/haar eruitziet.
- Vraag wat hij/zij zoal in zijn/haar vrije tijd doet.
- Vraag ook naar hoe zijn/haar weekend er gemiddeld uitziet.
- Beantwoord daarna ook de vragen van je klasgenoot.
- Doe een voorstel om het komend weekend samen iets te gaan doen. Bedenk zelf iets leuks.
- Sluit het gesprek op een passende manier af.

- Jij begint het gesprek.
- Bereid je rol eerst even voor.

Acknowledgements

Text Theme 5, exercise 4: *www.indax.com/history.html and http://primaryhomeworkhelp.co.uk/india/general.htm*
Text Theme 5, Test Yourself, exercise 2 *www.adrenalinquarry.co.uk/giant-swing-cornwall/*
Bridging the Gap MBO, Administrative and clerical services, exercise 2 *www.businessmanagementdaily.com/45259/is-the-staff-burning-through-office-supplies-like-theres-no-tomorrow*